W9-DCT-321

Night had settled completely now. Lamps blazed along the street. Groups of men rode in, shouting and laughing. Others reeled drunkenly from one saloon door to another. A piano banged frantically up at the sky. From a distance came what sounded to be a crash of furniture. A fight, probably.

Fallon reached down and touched the star hanging on his shirt. It felt slightly cold. A piece of tin. It meant seventy dollars a month, and nothing more. In half a dozen towns he had worn a badge. In a hundred other towns he had looked into the eyes of people and seen nothing but mean selfishness. Longhorn was no different from the rest. And it would be dangerous to let the gleam of a girl's copper hair convince him otherwise.

He reminded himself that he had a job to do.

Methodically, he hoisted his suitcase onto the desk and unpacked his gun.

Wear A
Fast Gun

by
JOHN JAKES

ace books
A Division of Charter Communications Inc.
A GROSSET & DUNLAP COMPANY
1120 Avenue of the Americas
New York, New York 10036

WEAR A FAST GUN

Copyright ©, 1956, by John Jakes

An Ace Book, by arrangement with the author.

To
My Parents
and
My Children

Printed in U.S.A.

CHAPTER I

ELI FALLON, commonly called Reb, did not know a solitary soul in Longhorn when he first arrived there. But in less than sixty minutes, he had shot a man to death.

The six-thirty via the capital crossed the eastern border of the Washoe Basin under a flood of yellowish light from an early evening sky. Its whistle cut across the rich cattle land near the town, signaling the approach. Dark clouds, their bellies stained a butter color, squeezed the evening glow down to a solitary bar over the hills to the west. In the smoking car, Fallon leaned back against the green velvet cushions, one foot propped on the seat opposite, and regarded the landscape shuttling by with eyes distinguished only by what at first glance seemed to be a kind of inhuman concern. He smoked a genuine Havana cigar, of dark tobacco, with an expensive aroma.

The conductor of the train heard the whistle's cry with pleasure. He lived in Longhorn. Soon he would be home with his wife and family; a pleasant thought. Secretively,

1

from his position at the end of the car, he threw a glance at the stranger with the cigar. Hadn't he seen that face before, in a drawing which accompanied a newspaper story that had to do with a bloody shooting in one of the cow towns farther west?

As he gazed at the stranger, he was caught short when the man whipped his head around and stared straight at him. The conductor quailed inwardly—why, he didn't know—and hastily went out onto the platform. Something about the stranger terrified him. Perhaps it was the apparent utter lack of feeling in the man's gray-blue eyes.

The train swung around a bend. The wind smelled of rich grass. The wheels clacked eagerly. The conductor knew most of the people in Longhorn, but he didn't know the stranger. And the railroad went no farther than the town. This line ran down from the capital, connecting with the east. Track had been laid after the war, when the cattle industry boomed, and the Washoe Basin took its place as one of the richest cattle lands in the West.

Say! Could the stranger be the new sheriff everyone had been talking about when he left? Maybe. Now he was sure about the face in the drawing. He thought of the man's face again. He shivered. Up ahead, a few outlying buildings began to appear.

Inside the car, Fallon sat erect, rose, walked down the aisle and threw his cigar in a spittoon. He returned to his seat, took down his bag from the luggage rack and headed for the platform. The conductor shied aside when Fallon stepped into the wind. Fallon watched shipping pens for cattle begin to flick by, jammed with steers. They bawled at the chuffing locomotive. The conductor muttered, "Excuse me," and ducked into the coach.

The train slowed, came to a halt, sparks mushrooming from the funnel-shaped stack. Fallon stepped down, the only passenger. The depot lay at one end of what was evidently the main street. The dusty thoroughfare was lined on both sides with the usual collection of false fronts: stores and offices, and a large number of saloons. The hitchrails were crowded. Light spilled into the street. The chorus of male laughs and shouts, mingled with a few tinny female voices, was nearly deafening in the still evening. Fallon moved away from the depot. He did not bother to move over to a sidewalk, but strode down the middle of the street, swinging his eyes right and then left evenly, getting the lay of the land.

Two men pitched brawling out of a saloon door and continued their fight in the dust. Fallon's eyes noted this. He walked on.

A woman briskly crossed the street in front of him. A small boy in overalls lagged behind. Fallen stopped the boy.

"Where's the sheriff's office, son?"

"What? Oh, the next block down. On the left. There's a sign outside."

Fallon started off. "Thanks."

"Are you the new sheriff?"

"Yes."

"Gee!" The boy's eyes rounded.

"Morris! Come here this instant!"

The woman's voice had an apprehensive sound. The boy hurried off to join his mother, who gave his elbow a sharp tug in reproof, and then cast a frightened look over her shoulder at Fallon's back. A sudden, peculiar fear had filled her when she looked into that man's face.

Fallon walked slowly, though with assurance. He carried his shoulders high and well back. His New England Yankee mother had named him Eli, not knowing that the name's original meaning, "high," would be so thoroughly carried out in her son's eventual six-foot-two frame. Oldsters drowsing on the veranda of the town's biggest hotel perked up when Fallon passed.

They saw a man whose height accentuated his slimness. The man wore a dark blue suit of eastern cut, and a derby hat, and had a pair of drooping sandy mustaches. The voices of the old men buzzed on the porch:

"Derby hat. You can allus tell 'em."

"That's got to be him. Word was, he'd be in on the six-thirty."

"Well, he looks like a trigger artist, right enough."

"Trigger artist! Did you get a look at them eyes o' his when he passed? Enough to give a man the chills. He looks like a born killer to me," was the final positive assertion. The tall man in the derby, carrying a suitcase, had already reached the next block and turned in toward the sidewalk.

CHAPTER II

BESIDE the door of a one story frame building, a sign had been tacked which read, *Sheriff*. Below it, in smaller letters: *R. Fallon*. Looking closely at it a moment, Fallon noticed the faded traces of other letters beneath the freshly painted ones that spelled out his name. Other names had been painted there before his. But that came as no surprise. The telegram had let him know what to expect.

Behind the window of the office, he could see a number of people waiting uncomfortably. Fallon opened the door and went in. Half a dozen heads turned to look at him. Fallon set down his bag. The men had the stiff look of ranchers dressed unwillingly in their Sunday church suits. A brief, uncomfortable pause ensued. Fallon noticed he had miscounted. There were only five men. The sixth person was a young woman.

She stood toward the back of the group, surveying him carefully. Fallon judged her to be in her middle twenties. Coppery hair hung down to her shoulders. Her eyes were gray and alert, and the full-skirted cotton dress could not conceal the fine lines of her figure. Fallon appraised her briefly, and the girl colored slightly in resentment. Not so sophisticated as some of the belles of St. Louis and elsewhere. Clean-scrubbed cheeks. Fresh air sort. But handsome.

He returned his attention to a stout, gray-haired rancher in his fifties who stepped forward with the air of group chairman. Fallon noted the strong resemblance between this man's features and those of the girl.

"Mr. Fallon?" The rancher extended his hand.

"That's right." Fallon shook hands.

"I'm Asa Wheeler, chairman of the town council. You certainly got here mighty fast."

"As soon as your telegram reached me in St. Louis, I got on a train."

"Well," spoke up a small man with no hair, "even a job as sheriff of a wild town like this is better than no job at all, eh, Mr. Fallon?"

"Correct," Fallon said. A trace of a smile played around his lean lips.

"These here are the other members of the town council." Wheeler performed the introductions. The bald man, also a rancher, was named Hawkins. The other three men were businessmen of the town. "You may think it's kind o' odd," Wheeler went on. "I mean, me and Hawkins taking an interest in having a clean, decent town here in Longhorn. My spread's out in the basin, but all the ranchers send their kids to school here in town, and our churches are trying to get started here, and we do all our business here, what with the pens down by the tracks, and . . ." Wheeler chuckled. "I shouldn't be so danged mouthy."

6

"I get the point," Fallon admitted.

"You forgot the most important member of the council, Asa," Hawkins said, trying to maintain his humorous role.

"Guess I did at that. Sheriff—I'll call you sheriff from now on—this is my daughter, Kate Wheeler, representing the women of the basin."

"How do you do?" Fallon said politely, inclining his head toward her.

"We've heard a great deal about your powers with a gun, Mr. Fallon," the girl said with cool reserve.

"Lordy, don't make the man brag, Kate!" Hawkins chortled. The others laughed. "Reb Fallon's name is recommend enough. Why, any man who could clean up Hayes Point and Meadville, two of the wildest, orneriest cow towns in the sta . . ."

"Let's concentrate on my job in Longhorn," Fallon said.

"That's right!" Wheeler chimed in. "Let's make Mr. Fallon feel right to home." Fallon's mouth again curved in a tight smile at this. Wheeler led the way through a door at the rear of the room. Along a corridor at the rear of the building ran a row of four cells. "We've got enough bad birds in Longhorn to keep these filled most of the time, Fallon," the stocky rancher told him. "What we've needed all along is a man who could get the ornery varmints *inside* the cells, before they get him."

"Don't get Asa wrong," another council member put in. "Longhorn's no Hayes Point or Meadville. We don't get the trail herds up from Texas here, but . . ."

"What he means is," Wheeler said, "that we don't

have a killin' once a day. Only once every two or three.'' The rancher was grim, not humorous. "But that's too many.''

Fallon nodded. "I understand. Now, about the salary. The telegram said . . .''

"Seventy dollars a month, plus room and board,'' spoke up Hawkins.

"The price of a gun is high,'' Kate Wheeler said dryly.

"That's right, it is,'' Fallon replied.

Asa Wheeler slapped Fallon's shoulder. "Sheriff, get yourself a bite to eat, and drop your things at the boarding house. Mrs. Clay's place. Anyone in town can tell you where it is. Then, in the morning, you can start making Longhorn into the kind of town we want it to be: decent and quiet.'' Two sharp gunshots, echoing from some distant alley, grimly punctuated his sentence.

"I could use that bite to eat,'' Fallon said. "By the way, is there a general store still open?''

"The Emporium's open till nine,'' another council member offered.

"Good. I want to buy some new clothes. St. Louis fashions aren't much good out here. But as for starting my job in the morning, Mr. Wheeler—well, I think I'll start tonight instead. A bad town cuts loose after sundown. All the crooks are too tired to do much during the day. I'll make the rounds of the saloons right after I eat and visit the Emporium.''

"Fine!'' Wheeler exclaimed. To the others on the council, he said: "I think we've got ourselves a real sheriff.''

"Mr. Fallon!''

Kate Wheeler stepped forward. Fallon faced her squarely.

"Yes?"

"I'm afraid Dad is a little too timid . . ."

"Aw now, Kate . . . sssh!"

"Dad, I'm sorry, but this needs saying."

"Go right ahead, Miss Wheeler." Fallon's voice dropped to a low key.

"The name Reb Fallon has become synonymous out here with gunfighter. You may wear a badge and act in the name of the law, but you have a reputation for liking a shooting brawl."

"I'm no iron man, Miss Wheeler. I've never been in a gunfight without having a tight, scared feeling in my belly. That may surprise you."

"It does," Kate Wheeler replied curtly.

"Nevertheless, it's true. The man who comes out on top in a gunfight is the man who controls his fear, who doesn't let it get the better of him."

"Be that as it may," Kate returned, "they say you've started gunfights before."

Fallon's anger stirred a little. "Every man who totes a badge in a tough town gets stories built up about him. That goes with the profession."

The girl smiled thinly. Her dislike for Fallon as a sort of hired mercenary was obvious. "You call killing a profession, then."

"I call being a lawman a profession. I'm not the only man who does it."

"Now see here, Kate . . ." Asa Wheeler began, attempting to be firm.

"Dad, you know I've got nothing against Mr. Fallon personally . . ."

"Thank you," Fallon returned. The girl's eyes blazed for a moment, but she regained control of herself.

9

"I merely want you to understand, Mr. Fallon, that we want this town cleaned up. That is not an excuse for useless gunplay. You've been hired to weed out the troublemakers in Longhorn, not to enhance your own reputation. People in the Washoe Basin want peace, not carnage."

"And I'll tell you right back, Miss Wheeler," Fallon spoke up hotly, "that you don't corral troublemakers by making a polite bow and saying 'please.' "

"This has gone far enough!" Asa Wheeler intervened.

"I second that," said Hawkins.

The girl seemed a bit crestfallen, but she accepted the authority of her father's words. She stepped back. "All right, Dad. I wanted to make sure Mr. Fallon knew how we felt."

"Mr. Fallon knows." Wheeler nodded his head quickly, to salve the situation. He fumbled in his vest pocket for a moment. Fallon met the girl's gaze again, and she flushed a second time, turning away.

"Here it is," Wheeler said, producing a metal star from his pocket. He made as if to pin it on Fallon's shirt, then chuckled embarrassedly and held it out to Fallon. "Here, Sheriff. You put it on yourself." The new sheriff pinned on his star.

"Council meeting is held every other Wednesday night," Hawkins informed him. "You can sort of give us an official report at those meetings."

Wheeler frowned slightly. "Fallon, this won't be an easy job. The boys from Luke Mitchell's ranch alone account for plenty of trouble. Then we've got the night riders to cope with, and . . ." Wheeler raised his gaze, serious beneath thick, grizzled brows. "But then you'll find out about the situation soon enough. There's one thing I didn't tell you in the telegram. We've had three sheriffs in Longhorn in the past year. They're all buried in the town cemetery. So you have your job cut out for you."

Fallon said nothing.

Wheeler fumbled with his hat, uncomfortable in his official role. "Well, gents, we'd better mosey, and let the sheriff get his dinner."

The members of the council called out words of encouragement as they left the office. Kate Wheeler lingered behind, a slight frown puckering her brows.

"Something more you wanted to tell me, Miss Wheeler?"

"I . . . well, I didn't mean to sound so sharp when I spoke up. But I did want to make my position clear," she added firmly. "I have nothing personal against you," she repeated.

He smiled. "That's nice to hear. Why do you look so startled?"

"A real smile! I wondered if you had it in you."

Fallon perched easily on the corner of the desk, unable to keep a tinge of bitterness from his words. "I smile when there's a reason. With the world the way it is, I seldom find a reason."

"Perhaps you haven't looked hard enough."

"Perhaps," he echoed slowly, "I've looked *too* hard."

Her frown deepened. "You're a puzzling man, Mr. Fallon."

"Don't try to understand me. You wouldn't like the way I think."

11

Almost with regret, she said, "I'm afraid you might be right. Good night, Mr. Fallon." And she swept out the door to join her father and the other men, who were lighting cigars and talking enthusiastically. Their voices drifted away. Fallon went to the window, and saw Kate Wheeler and her father climb into a buggy and head out of town. He stared after them a moment. It can never be any different, he thought. She's like all the rest. So be careful. Don't stare at that copper hair of hers too hard, or those eyes, or that figure. With a sharp exclamation of dismay, he turned away from the window.

Night had settled completely now. Lamps blazed along the street. Groups of men rode in, shouting and laughing. Others reeled drunkenly from one saloon door to another. A piano banged frantically up at the sky. From a distance came what sounded to be a crash of furniture. A fight, probably.

Fallon reached down and touched the star hanging on his shirt. It felt slightly cold. A piece of tin. It meant seventy dollars a month, and nothing more. In half a dozen towns he had worn a badge. In a hundred other towns he had looked into the eyes of people and seen nothing but mean selfishness. Longhorn was no different from the rest. And it would be dangerous to let the gleam of a girl's copper hair convince him otherwise.

He reminded himself that he had a job to do.

Methodically, he hoisted his suitcase onto the desk and unpacked his gun.

CHAPTER III

AT THE Emporium Department Store, Fallon purchased a pair of dark trousers, a vest, a shirt and a flat-crowned gray hat. He carried his parcel into a deserted restaurant next door, where he wolfed beef and brown gravy, potatoes, thick slices of freshly baked bread and several cups of strong, acid coffee. It became apparent that the trouble in Longhorn centered in the saloons lining both sides of the street. This, he knew from experience, was not unusual. Well, there would have to be a few rules laid down. Hastily he finished his after-dinner cigar, leaving it half smoked. He left the restaurant. As always, he felt coldly curious about the strength of the opposition. He wanted to appraise that, and quickly.

At the office, he changed clothes and took his gun belt from a lower drawer in the desk. The weapon was a six-shot Colt, undistinguished except for its gleaming, well-cared-for appearance. He slid the gun part way out of the worn leather holster and massaged the

grainy oaken butt. That had a solid feel. He could depend
on it. He began to whistle as he buckled on the gun belt,
tying the holster to his right thigh so that the butt touched
the mid-point of his lower arm when the arm hung free and
relaxed. Blowing out the lamp, Fallon closed the office
door and stood a moment on the sidewalk, inhaling the
warm air that smelled of lathered horses. The quiet night
sky arched high above the town, studded with the peaceful
diamond points of stars. In contrast, blatant yellow lamplight, filled with turgid clouds of smoke, boiled out the
door of a saloon opposite.

Fallon crossed the street. A couple of cowpunchers,
arguing hotly just outside the saloon door, cut off their talk
sharply and treated him to a curious gaze as he passed.
Fallon walked rapidly now. He straight-armed the bat-
wings open with a flat smack of his palm and stepped
through. Men turned to look at him. The busy activity of
the gambling tables ceased for a moment. Talk died
briefly, so that the player piano sounded all the louder. A
pair of frowzy girls in cheap spangled dresses eyed Fallon
professionally. His restless gaze roamed through the long,
smoky room, taking in a dozen details. He did not miss the
antagonistic looks from one or two of the card dealers.
Fallon had lived this scene before: the furtive glances at
his face and gun; the swift mental appraisal by a dozen
different brains in one room of potential draw speed; the
question as to whether things might be tough from now on.
Once again feeling the tightening in his belly which meant
that his nerves were attuned to possible trouble, Fallon
walked to the long bar stretching along the wall. A bartender with a curl of hair oiled down to his forehead did not
raise his eyes from the beer tap as he asked:

"Yours?"

"I want to see the boss."

"He's busy."

"Get him."

The bartender continued to concentrate on the beer hissing from the tap into a schooner. "Look, if you want a drink, speak up. Otherwise . . ." At this moment, the bartender drew the brimming schooner from under the tap and raised his eyes. He looked at Fallon's badge, and then at his face.

Fallon put both hands on the edge of the bar.

"I said get the boss."

Without a word, the bartender whirled and disappeared toward the rear of the room. He talked quickly to a burly, mustached man also wearing a bar apron who was tending near the back. The burly individual walked back to where Fallon stood, wiping his hands on his apron. Wary suspicion gleamed in his small eyes.

"Evening, Sheriff. You wanted to see me?"

"That's right. You run this place?"

"I own it, yeah. Why?" A half-veiled contempt gleamed in the burly man's eyes.

"Because I want to come to an understanding."

Suspicion deepened. "Understanding?"

"A man who can't hold his liquor is liable to go for his gun, and for no good reason. So I want you to clamp down on proddy drunks. Any man who's had too much and wants more, you refuse to serve him. Order the rest of your bartenders to do the same. Then bounce him. See that he gets dumped in the horse trough outside. You've got a bouncer, haven't you?"

"I bounce 'em myself," the burly man grumbled.

''Well, then, see that you do it.''

''Looky here, Sheriff,'' the other complained. ''My business is selling liquor, not runnin' a temperance society. . . .''

''And my business,'' Fallon returned evenly, ''is seeing that a bunch of crazy drunks don't shoot up innocent citizens. You won't lose money. I'll hold you personally responsible for the conduct of men when they're in here. If they get too tough, send for me. That's part of my job too. But I think I ought to remind you,'' Fallon added quietly, ''that you'll make no money at all if I close you up, and I'll do it the first time a man who's drunk too much of your liquor gets out of hand. What I'm asking's reasonable, I think.''

''Reasonable, nothing!'' the man growled. ''It's plumb crazy.'' He poked a meaty index finger in Fallon's direction. ''I don't like what you're telling me, Sheriff, and you're acting like an upstart. I'll let you in on this much: folks in this town don't cotton to interference with business, 'specially saloon keepers, and 'specially when the interference comes from a green badge toter.'' The owner's cheeks had grown purple with rage. ''You figure you got a lot of authority, wearing that piece o' tin?''

''This isn't the first time I've worn a star, if that's what you mean.''

The burly man sniggered. ''Oh, sure.''

''Maybe you haven't heard. My name's Fallon.''

The words, spoken softly, as a fact, with no hint of conceit in them, struck the burly man like a sledgehammer fist in the face. ''Fallon?'' he repeated. ''*Reb* Fallon?''

''That's what it says on the sign across the street. Now, do I get cooperation?''

16

The burly man appraised Fallon in a new light. Reluctantly, backing down, he scratched his chin and scowled. He gazed vacantly out beyond Fallon's shoulder, not wanting to meet the sheriff's eyes. "I'll pass the word to my boys," he muttered.

"Good. Now I'll take a whisky."

Abruptly, talk which had died off during the interchange commenced again. Fallon sipped from the shot glass, relaxing a bit as the raw liquid slid down his throat and exploded warmly in his belly. The owner of the saloon, displeased but cowed, was already issuing instructions to the other bartenders. Fallon listened to the conversation of his neighbors at the bar. Speculation was rife concerning the new sheriff's character, and it was openly voiced. Fallon turned, surveyed the tables once more, and walked toward the street.

From behind him, someone called, "He won't buffalo Luke Mitchell and his boys that easy."

Fallon did not bother to look around. A few timid laughs followed him out through the swinging doors. He cut toward the left, to the next saloon on the street, which was called the Boston. The establishment was doing a brisk, though not a booming business. The crowd seemed a little different from that Fallon had seen in the previous place: here, more oldsters sat absorbed in games of stud or faro, not drinking. Only a relative handful of armed cowhands were present. There were no girls to be seen anywhere. Fallon immediately checked off the Boston as a lesser trouble spot. But he asked for the manager nevertheless, and learned that he was out at the moment. Fallon passed his order along to the bartender, who did not seem displeased about it.

17

"Mr. Nash'll be glad to hear things are settling down some," the bartender informed Fallon.

"Nash?"

"Mr. Tom Nash, of Cambridge, Mass." The man grinned. "Went to some university up there. A real educated gent."

Fallon left the Boston, a little surprised to hear that the saloon owner was an educated Easterner. But then, Fallon recalled, he had run across far stranger specimens in his travels. Rich ground, whether there was gold beneath its surface or grass on top of it, attracted men from every part of the country, a good many of them lawless. As Fallon paused on the sidewalk outside the Boston, he noted that the street seemed to have quieted slightly. Perhaps the word was being passed. Well, that was all to the good.

He made the rounds of eleven other saloons, both large and small, and his orders were greeted with every response from a shrug to a vehement curse. But most owners on the street now knew his name, and though they grumbled, they did not rebel openly. As Fallon walked across the street toward the only saloon he had not visited, he reflected that he should have been flattered by the way men perked up when they heard his name. Strangely, he was not. The satisfaction was an empty one.

This last saloon appeared to be the largest of the lot. An ornately painted sign stretching all the way across the roof of the porch labeled the establishment as the Crystal. The din coming from the open door was thunderous. Voices grated more harshly here. Laughs sounded more drunken. The first thing that struck Fallon's eyes as he stepped inside was the large number of girls, all of them overly painted, with calculating eyes. Great beds of blue smoke floated under a giant crystal chandelier hanging from the ceiling, whose prisms reflected the light of candles in multiple silver flashes. As Fallon passed from the front of the bar toward an empty spot at the rear, he noticed a tight group of men clinging together over their drinks. A man in a soiled hat and vest, face dotted by beard stubble, surveyed Fallon closely as he walked past. The man had a powerful, rangy frame which commanded attention, and his small dark eyes puckered close together in a glint of dumb animal cleverness. As Fallon moved on, he heard this man addressed as ''Luke'' by a thin man with a livid scar on the point of his chin.

Luke Mitchell? Wheeler had mentioned that a man named Mitchell headed a trouble-making bunch. The name had come up again at the first saloon. Fallon fixed the man's face firmly in mind as he walked.

The bartender directed him to a desk in a secluded corner at the rear of the room. There, a man who said he was the manager, but not the owner, received Fallon's orders with a sneer of contempt.

''Another thing,'' Fallon spoke.

''Hurry up, Sheriff. I'm busy.'' The manager riffled papers on his desk.

Fallon slammed his knuckles lightly on the desk top. ''You're not too busy to listen a minute longer.''

''I guess since you're the famous Reb Fallon, I'd better pay a mind to you,'' the manager said sarcastically.

''If I get any reports that these girls of yours are rolling the punchers, they'll go out of town so fast your head will spin.''

"I got it, Sheriff," the manager smirked. "Anything *else?*"

"No," Fallon said, stalking away. The whole atmosphere in the Crystal displeased him. Here were the hard-eyed men, the worn gun holsters that spelled trouble. He stopped at the rear end of the bar and ordered another whisky. He had the feeling that the town was on its good behavior tonight; the men wanted to find out what the new peace officer was like. But trouble rumbled ominously in the heavy air; Fallon had sensed it, somehow, when he noticed Luke Mitchell's careful scrutiny. For he didn't doubt that the stubble-chinned man was Mitchell, since he had collected such a group of followers around him, and was obviously a center of attention up at the head of the bar.

Leaning back against the bar, Fallon juggled his shot glass and surveyed the busy gambling tables. He noticed a puncher who had just come in and was now walking toward the bar. The man—he looked more like a boy —had a tiny frame, and an ugly, though not unpleasant face. He had a powerful torso, but Fallon saw that his legs were thin and stunted. One leg seemed a little shorter than the other. The puncher hardly came up to the shoulders of most men, but he carried his chest out, not in defiance, but in a kind of stubborn pride. The puncher limped as he walked.

Fallon watched. The tiny cowhand started past the Mitchell group, but one of the men caught his elbow and pulled him around; the one with the scarred chin. The tiny cowpoke's eyes blazed with anger, but the scar-jawed man pantomimed an invitation to an open spot at the bar,

20

which he made by pushing a couple of his companions to the side. The tiny man hesitated, looked around, saw how crowded the rest of the bar was, and reluctantly stepped up to the rail. As the tiny man ordered, the one with the scar on his chin glanced at Mitchell as if to say, *Watch this.* Mitchell threw back his head and laughed.

Fallon felt his stomach tighten again in warning. The situation did not look good. He set down his shot glass, walked down the bar and elbowed in again, a few spaces away from where the small puncher stood, surrounded by Mitchell's crew. Other men at the bar made a place for Fallon when they noticed his badge.

". . . Aw, come on, Piney," Fallon heard the scar-jawed man say. "Lemme buy you a drink."

"I'll buy my own, Bleeker," the man named Piney returned in a thin but strong voice.

"You heard him, Bleeker." Mitchell spoke with a coarse laugh.

"Sure, I forgot." Bleeker's words blurred thickly, drunkenly. "When Piney Woods from them old piney woods of Tennessee speaks, the whole world shuts up to listen." Fallon saw lines of anger tighten and convulse Piney's mouth. "Tell me, Piney," Bleeker went on, "do they run barefoot down in them hills? Maybe that's where you got that bum leg—stepped into somebody else's trap, eh, Piney?"

Piney's hands constricted on his shot glass. "I just came in here for a peaceable drink, Bleeker," he said with a noticeable drawl.

"Sure, o' course!" Bleeker laughed. He tossed off another shot himself. Mitchell stood watching in amusement. "Tell me, Piney, how'd you ever learn to ride a hoss, bein' such a mite? I'd think an old cow pony would go plumb crazy if you straddled him. He'd think a crippled calf had climbed . . ."

Piney swung around and threw the liquor straight into Bleeker's face.

Bleeker gasped in amazement, and then his face blurred into drunken lines, becoming hateful. "Back out of the way, boys," Luke Mitchell said, as if anticipating a little fun. Heads turned all over the saloon. Piney and Bleeker stood alone, facing one another. Bleeker reached up to the bar, seized a bottle by its neck, smashed it on the wood and hefted the ugly saw-toothed weapon. Pure rage gleamed in his eyes.

"It's about time somebody taught you a lesson," Bleeker said vengefully, moving forward.

Piney went for his gun. Bleeker stabbed the tiny puncher's gun hand with the broken bottle, bringing blood. Piney fumbled, but his gun would not come free. Bleeker clamped his left hand around the tiny man's throat and drew back his right to grind the bottle into the puncher's face. The glass points glittered wickedly in the light. Bleeker, at least forty pounds heavier than the other man, needed only a second longer. . . .

But in that second, Fallon moved.

He caught Bleeker's wrist in mid-air and tore the bottle loose, throwing it to the floor. Bleeker released Piney, who staggered backwards, massaging his throat and watching the scene with wide eyes. A couple of the Mitchell men surged forward, dropping their hands tentatively toward their guns, but Mitchell held them back with an outstretched arm, his eyes glinting warily.

Bleeker, a drunken madness in his eyes now, faced Fallon. "What are you buttin' in for, Sheriff?"

"You can do your fighting outside the town limits," Fallon told him. "And pick on a man your own size next time." Fallon felt the cold sweat on his palms. *It was coming. . . .*

"Get out of my way, Sheriff!"

"Don't be a fool. You're too drunk to pull that gun."

A wild scramble ensued, as men ducked for cover.

"I can outdraw any tinhorn badge toter any day of the week!" Bleeker cried. His whole frame quivered, taut, and he crouched slightly. Fallon's right arm tensed.

"Better listen to him, Sheriff," Luke Mitchell warned. "He's fast."

"Don't draw your gun . . ." Fallon warned the scar-jawed man.

Bleeker cursed, and his right hand blurred downward.

Fallon cleared leather and fired three shots in a single fluid motion. The second between the squeeze of the trigger and the report seemed like an eternity. Bleeker's gun dropped from his hand, unfired. His mouth gaped. His eyes saw the final horror of death, and glazed. He wanted to scream, but he couldn't. Almost without a sound, he crumpled to the floor; and the blood was beginning to come now, staining the holes in his shirt right over his heart.

CHAPTER IV

ACRID bluish smoke drifted between Fallon and the Mitchell men. Fallon gave Bleeker's hand a push, using the toe of his boot. The hand flopped limply over as the new sheriff slowly holstered his Colt. A half-dozen men had formed themselves into an angry knot behind the rangy Mitchell, and they waited now for orders from their chief. One of the gang scratched the fingernails of a tense, clawed hand along the side of his denims. The sound was surprisingly loud in the saloon. No one at the tables stirred. The scene had not yet played itself out.

Fallon, making an effort to control his fast breathing, swiftly figured the odds against him. Mitchell's eyes traveled back and forth from Bleeker's corpse to the sheriff in a tight black frown of puzzlement. The balance could tip either way. He might be facing seven guns in another second, depending upon how high Mitchell's emotional temperature had risen. Keeping his face as blank as stone, Fallon figured his strategy, in case the gunfight should come.

Another second ticked by. Then another.

Mitchell cleared his throat with a raspy, almost inaudible sound. A door opened and closed softly somewhere behind Fallon.

The puncher with the scratching fingernails suddenly blurted: "For Pete's sake, Luke . . ."

"*Shut up!*" said Mitchell.

Fallon stood in a relaxed position, waiting. You could never judge something like this accurately. The slightest movement might set Mitchell off.

Mitchell moved.

He put his left toe forward, but instead of touching Bleeker's hand, he used his boot to roll the corpse over, so that he didn't have to look at the suddenly pasty and utterly horrible death mask.

"A couple of you take him to Dilahanty's Funeral Parlor," Mitchell said between tight lips.

"Luke, are you gonna stand here and . . ." another of the gang began in a rage.

"Do like I say! Move!"

Mitchell's words were hardly above a whisper, but they were loaded with savagery. Some of the starch went out of his men. They shot glances at each other, sidewise, disgruntled. A couple of them stepped forward to get the body. As they leaned down to heft the corpse, they looked at Fallon.

Pure murder was in their eyes.

Fallon, breathing a bit easier, almost regretted that there had not been more gunplay. Because as surely as he lived, there would come another time when he would have to face these men. The looks of the two now lugging Bleeker's body toward the door told him that. They had never seen him before tonight, but they hated him; hated, really, the badge he wore. Fallon realized that Mitchell's men were gunslingers first, cowpunchers second. Fallon knew how to recognize the wolf eyes of utterly ruthless men.

Piney Woods, still massaging his throat, looked nervously at Fallon, then at Mitchell, and also walked toward the front door. He held his little frame erect. He wanted to hurry out of the saloon, but pride would not let him. The batwings flapped, closing. Mitchell turned toward the gaping spectators at the tables.

"What are all o' you looking at?" he demanded in a loud voice.

Like puppets, the card players and girls jerked into quick motion. As the hubbub rose again, Mitchell took a step forward.

"You didn't have to gun him down, Sheriff," he said threateningly.

"What was he going to do to me? Shake my hand?"

Mitchell's brows puckered together. His voice lowered to a growl. "You still had no call . . ."

"And I say I did. I told him to take his fight out of the town limits. Besides, the other one did not have a chance. The puncher with the game leg, I mean."

"Pfagh!" Mitchell made a spitting, contemptuous sound. The corner of his mouth twitched, but not humorously. "I'm sorry to see a real heroic jasper like you in Longhorn. The big hero on the white horse—is that what you aim to be, Sheriff?"

"I aim to keep this town quiet. That means trimming down anyone who thinks he's got a right to start shooting when he gets his toes stepped on. You might as well get that clear.''

Mitchell waved. ''Oh, I got it clear, right enough.'' Suddenly he stiffened. ''But I don't like it.''

One of Mitchell's men laughed, a shrill, whinnying sound. ''The famous Reb Fallon! Pulling iron on a drunk. . . .''

Fallon's eyes went down to slits. ''You want to try your luck?'' he asked the emaciated puncher quietly.

''Let me handle this, Simmonds,'' Mitchell rasped over his shoulders. Simmonds sneered but kept quiet.

''I guess you don't know very much about me, do you, Sheriff?'' Mitchell asked.

''I've heard enough to know you're a troublemaker.''

Mitchell could hardly control his rage. ''By gosh, I ought to cut you down right now!''

Fallon felt the sweat on his palms. ''Go ahead. You've got seven guns on your side; I've got one.'' His voice grew acid. ''Or would that look too much like plain murder to folks in this town? Seven against one might get you and your boys a rope, where nothing else would.''

Fallon saw he had scored a hit. For Mitchell, gazing quickly again at the still curious crowds around the tables, seemed to hesitate for a minute. He was not a man to worry about a reputation as a troublemaker, Fallon knew, but still, a gun battle with seven men on one side against a lone sheriff might put him in a really bad light.

''Maybe you'd like to go outside,'' Fallon suggested. ''We'll invite these folks for witnesses. I'll take you and your pack rats one at a time!'' The angry words broke forth, but Fallon did not want to call them back. He knew

27

these men would never take him up on a series of even gun fights. They might get him at night, but . . . Fallon pushed that thought hastily from his mind.

"You've crossed the wrong man, Sheriff," Mitchell said raggedly.

"Have I?"

"You wait and see. Come on, boys. The air in here's putrid."

Mitchell wheeled, and with his men following him, spurs clanking loudly on the floor, he slammed the bat-wings wide and strode into the night. A couple of seconds later, there came a brief, explosive rattle of hoofs, dying away gradually as the horsemen pounded out of town. Fallon, who had not had a chance to finish his drink earlier, ordered another, downed it, and started to leave. As he turned from the bar he noticed for the first time a man standing on the balcony which ran across the back of the room. The man, in his middle thirties, stood by the balcony rail, subjecting Fallon to careful scrutiny. He had a square, blocky face topped by yellowish hair, and wore a gray suit of expensive cut. Built on the massive lines of a slab of stone, the man still had a stubborn, shrewdly intelligent gaze. Fallon wondered who the man was, but speculation was cut short on this matter as he stepped onto the darkened saloon porch.

Someone moved from the shadows, causing Fallon to whirl around and start for his gun.

The figure stepped into the light which fell through one of the saloon windows.

It was Piney Woods, the limping cowhand, with a sheepish grin spread across his gnarled features.

"Sorry if I spooked you, Sheriff," he said in his drawling tone.

"S'all right. I didn't expect to be meeting anyone out here, that's all."

The small man scuffed one boot embarrassedly. "I wanted to say thanks for what happened in there." Fallon gazed uncomfortably away from the man's appreciative gaze.

"Forget it."

"No, I can't forget it! That Bleeker would have had me in another minute, and I know it. That Mitchell outfit is plumb full of mean, twisty cusses who won't give a feller an even chance."

Fallon, even more uncomfortable, began, "Look here . . ."

"Woods is the name, Piney Woods. That name's sort of a joke, being I'm from Tennessee." He stuck out his hand. Reluctantly, Fallon shook it. "I work out at the Wheeler spread." Piney spat with contempt. "Mr. Wheeler says I'm a good hand, but trash like that Mitchell outfit think all I'm good for is to be pushed around. Ordinarily," Piney poked out a finger for emphasis, "I'd be sore if I didn't get to fight my own battles. But when Reb Fallon stops it . . . well, all I can do is say thanks."

Fallon warmed momentarily to the man's appreciation. There was something admirable in the bearing of this little fellow, who acted like more of a man than some Fallon had known. But as always, the old unsureness, the old distrust got the better of Fallon. He said,

"I didn't do you any special favors, Piney. My job is to keep peaceful people from getting gunned down. I get paid for it.'' He finished curtly, ''And I don't want any special thanks.''

Baffled and hurt by the curt rebuff, Piney Woods stepped back. He forced a grin. ''Sorry, Mr. Fallon, I . . .'' He could say no more.

''Let's forget about it,'' Fallon repeated. He gave his hat brim a firm pull. ''Be seeing you.'' And he stepped into the street and headed back toward his office. Once he turned—he did not know why—and saw the little man still standing under the light of the window, saddened and perplexed.

CHAPTER V

BLAST IT, Fallon thought as he walked. What was the tiny puncher trying to do? Set him up as some kind of god? Recalling the awe-struck, almost worshipful look in Piney's face, Fallon writhed inwardly. Why did people have to take a gesture like the fight in the saloon for more than it was worth? His thoughts took a bitter twist. Sure enough, Piney Woods probably had a rugged time keeping his place as a cowhand, with his bad leg and all. But now, Fallon said to himself, I suppose he thinks what I did entitles him to tell all his cronies that Reb Fallon, the gunfighter, is his personal friend!

That last was wrong somehow, but it bothered him to think about it.

He arrived at the office and concentrated on cleaning out the desk. The remaining personal effects of the last sheriff, a man named Eberts, he threw into a wastebasket. The clock on the wall ticked loudly. He sat down, raised his boots to the desk and smoked a cigar. Time went by. A man came from one of the saloons, requesting help. A puncher had ridden his horse in through the front door. Fallon went to the saloon, arrested the puncher, saw that the horse was taken outside again, and herded the puncher back to jail. The man came peaceably enough, laughing and saying with the utmost seriousness, "Thanks, Sheriff. When I get likkered, I'm no good; I'm just a ring-tailed bobcat and I know it." When Fallon locked him in the cell, the man continued to thank him, then began to sing sad songs about his dear old mother back in Ireland.

At a few minutes before eleven the office door opened. In walked the man Fallon had seen on the balcony at the Crystal.

At close range, the man's heavy hands showed a brutal power. But Fallon saw at once the light of a calculating intelligence glittering in the depths of his greenish eyes.

"Evening, Sheriff," the man said in a smooth voice. "I thought I'd drop in and introduce myself." He stuck his hand forward. "Mace Coldfield's the name. I own the Crystal Saloon."

"Have a chair."

Coldfield settled himself and crossed his legs. Fallon sat down again too, studying his visitor. Coldfield smiled pleasantly, but the smile was so much paint slapped for effect on a chunk of rock.

"Anything special on your mind?" Fallon inquired.

Coldfield frowned slightly. "As a matter of fact, yes. I was in the back of my office, upstairs in the Crystal, when the disturbance took place tonight. So I didn't get to see it. Sheriff, I wanted to come over here and tell you that I'm sorry trouble got started in my place. My manager told me

of the new ruling you'd laid down, and I think it's fine.''
Some of the flintiness came through Coldfield's pose of
good humor. "Up to a point."

"There's no 'point' about it," Fallon returned pleasantly. "I'm going to enforce it, that's all."

"You're only one man, though." Coldfield chuckled.

"There are others to back me up. But I don't think
that'll be necessary."

"I suppose you're right. But keep in mind, too, Sheriff,
that men around here are used to drinking plenty of liquor.
Why, most of the leather-hided cowpokes in this basin
have poured down so much whisky they've forgotten what
it feels like to be drunk. They can hold it."

"Mitchell's man Bleeker couldn't. He's dead now because he couldn't."

Coldfield studied his fingernails. Carefully he said,
"I'm sure Luke Mitchell had no direct hand in the business."

"He stood by and let Bleeker badger that little fellow."

A faint smile of contempt curved Coldfield's lips.
"Come now, Fallon. After all, that cripple . . ."

"Whether Woods is a cripple or not has got nothing to
do with it. Bleeker thought he could get away with rough-
ing him up because Woods couldn't fight back. Ideas like
that can make a town run wild. I've seen it happen."

Coldfield shook his head, frowning. "I'm on your side,
all the way. But you know by now that Luke Mitchell
doesn't take to being pushed."

"Bleeker called the play; I didn't."

"Yes," Coldfield returned smoothly. "But again, it's
all in how you look at it."

Fallon distrusted Mace Coldfield: distrusted the expensive, polished front which concealed something else Coldfield could not quite keep out of his manner.

"Coldfield, are you by any chance trying to warn me against tangling with Mitchell and his outfit any more?"

"Warn you? Why on earth would I do that?"

"I don't know, right at the moment. Maybe Mitchell's a personal friend of yours."

"No, he's not." Coldfield shook his head, but Fallon thought he did it too quickly. Now the saloon owner was all business. "What happens to Mitchell and his boys is no concern of mine. What I *am* interested in is keeping my business going. I don't want the saloon trade in Longhorn to die off altogether."

"Do you mean that Mitchell swings that much influence? If he gets scared off, so will everyone else?"

"The devil with Mitchell!" Coldfield snapped.

Fallon shrugged. "Anyway, he won't get any special consideration."

Coldfield leaned back in his chair and slowly lit a cigar. The lamp on the desk threw fierce pinpoints into his chill green eyes. "You know, Fallon, you have a way of twisting a man's words that could be displeasing."

Fallon lost patience. "I'm not in a popularity contest. You're after something. Now what is it?"

Coldfield's mouth smiled. His eyes did not. He waved his cigar. "All right, I'll play it your way. My manager told me what you said about my girls. And that business about drunks getting obnoxious . . . well, the more liquor I sell, the more money I make. I like making money. I have a wife who likes to have me make money. I'll go along with you, part way. But don't expect to turn my place into a church.''

"If I do?''

"Fallon, we're a couple of grown men. I don't have to make melodramatic hints. You've been in towns like this before.'' He inhaled his cigar deeply. "Step on my toes—I'll step back. That should be clear.''

"That part is.''

"What do you mean?''

"I know you may think I'll cut off some of your business. But that's still a pretty thin excuse for coming all the way over here. That long-nosed manager of yours could have warned me off just as easy.'' A death's head grin sat on Fallon's mouth. "You know, Mr. Coldfield, since you're being so frank, I think you're interested in me for some other reason. Maybe you're afraid of me. If you are, you've made a stupid play, because I don't know what you're driving at.''

Coldfield stood up, dropped his cigar, and smashed it out under his heel. "Afraid?'' He shook his head decisively. "No. Not of one man. Not of a piece of tin that says sheriff.'' Coldfield's eyes narrowed. "You may be closer to the truth than you think. Don't push the line of reasoning too far. It might not be wise.'' Coldfield touched his hat brim mockingly. "Good evening, Sheriff.'' He vanished into the night.

CHAPTER VI

ONE afternoon while Fallon was returning to his office, he glanced across the street to see Mace Coldfield talking to a woman in a buggy. The buggy, a fancy affair with cushioned seats, yellow wheel spokes and red leather dashboard, had an eastern air about it, down to the pair of bays in the traces. They appeared to be blooded animals. And the expensive vehicle fitted perfectly the woman on the seat to whom Coldfield was talking. Fallon paused a moment, struck by the dark, fiery intensity of the woman's beauty. Her yellow hat and the yellow gown hugging her slender, high-breasted figure set off the ebony sheen of her hair and the haughty, patrician face. The full, ripe curve of her red mouth contrasted with the china-like delicacy of her skin.

The conversation completed, Coldfield turned brusquely away and stalked back into the Crystal. Aware she was being watched, the woman swung her head around slowly to gaze at Fallon over the bed of a buckboard rattling by in the dust. Her gaze contained first curiosity, then veiled admiration. The ripe lips pouted briefly in a secretive smile. She picked up the reins, called softly to the team, and the expensive buggy moved smoothly off down the street.

She appeared fragile . . . yes, even unhealthy.

Curious, Fallon turned to an old man seated on a bench in front of a general store. "Who was that woman that just drove off?"

The old-timer snickered. "Coldfield's wife. Miz India Coldfield. A reg'lar queen around these parts. Coldfield brought her out from the East a year or two ago."

"She's attractive," Fallon commented.

"Shore she is. But she's a worse drunk than half the punchers in the basin."

Startled, Fallon frowned. "What?"

The oldster sucked on a corncob pipe. "Didn't you see her weavin' around on the buggy seat? Drinks like a fish all the time. Coldfield's got a job on his hands to handle her. No sir." The old-timer shook his head sagely. "Sometimes it just don't pay to have a woman too good-lookin', 'specially not in this country."

Fallon moved on.

A day or two later, while riding around the town, Fallon passed a house which someone pointed out as Coldfield's. A large, two-story affair, it was set back from the street on a broad lawn. It had an expensive air about it, like the buggy. Velvet drapes hung in the windows. Fallon could see a separate stable and buggy house at the rear. As he rode by, he thought he saw someone standing in a down-stairs window. The drapes fell quickly back in place, and sun bouncing off the window glass made it impossible for him to see more. But Fallon was sure India Coldfield had been watching him.

Word drifted into town at the beginning of the next week that the night riders had struck again, running off three hundred head of prime beef from a ranch on the outlying fringe of the basin. The night riders were a crew of rustlers, supposedly from over the hills to the west of the basin, who wore bleached feed sacks over their heads, and who rode in the night, striking frequently and taking advantage of the lack of any sort of organization on the part of the ranchers themselves. This problem properly fell within Fallon's jurisdiction, and he knew he would have to deal with it eventually, even though the ranchers did not seem able to get up enough gumption to organize a protective counterattacking force.

Fallon heard this news late one afternoon, in one of the saloons. He was pondering the problem as he returned to his office, when he suddenly stumbled against someone, and glanced up hastily. Kate Wheeler drew back, ruffled. Fallon grinned.

"Clumsy of me, Miss Wheeler."

"That's quite all right, Mr. Fallon." She surveyed him coolly. "Well, you seem to be living up to your reputation."

"I don't quite follow . . ."

"You killed Luke Mitchell's man, Bleeker, didn't you?"

Fallon's gaze grew hard. "He had it coming."

"Did he? Perhaps. Certain people, however, say that it was not absolutely necessary for you to kill him."

"I do my job as I see it."

A thin smile touched the girl's lips. "Undoubtedly. It's a pity that your way is so violent. Good afternoon, Mr. Fallon."

And she swept on down the sidewalk, the late afternoon sunlight throwing lustrous copper glints into her hair. Blast her anyway! Fallon thought wrathfully. Couldn't she understand that bringing law to a town demanded weapons other than polite requests? Immediately, he suggested to himself that he was wrought up because he could not dismiss his interest in the Wheeler girl. Then the other side of his mind countered with the eternal bitter charge: *she's no different from the rest*. Thoughtfully lighting a cigar, Fallon walked slowly along the sidewalk, uneasy, disturbed, and wishing he could settle things in his mind.

When Fallon stepped in the door of his office, he saw that he had a visitor. The man rose and stepped forward to introduce himself. "Nash is the name, Sheriff. Tom Nash."

Fallon shook the man's hand. His visitor was in his early forties; the high shock of dark hair rising from the forehead showed streaked touches of silver. Nash stood just under six feet, and had small hands and feet. Above the shirt bosom which shone with the gleaming whiteness of immaculate linen, Fallon saw a slender, almost cadaverous, thoroughly intelligent face. Nash had the look of an ascetic, but the Colt on his hip appeared well used.

"Have a chair, Mr. Nash," Fallon invited. "You're the owner of the Boston, aren't you?"

"Correct." Nash seated himself with ease. Each

movement he made showed perfect assurance and control. His voice was smooth and calm. "I happened to be out when you made your first call, but I've been meaning to drop by ever since, and thank you."

"Thank me?" Fallon took a cigar from his desk drawer, lit it. "What for?"

"For issuing that order for saloon owners to refuse to serve unruly drunks. I'm grateful for that ruling, believe me. Only a week before you arrived, there was a fight in my place, and before I managed to stop it, the drunken fools had broken up three hundred dollars worth of furniture and equipment. Longhorn has been a good deal quieter since you arrived."

"Too quiet, maybe," Fallon murmured. When Nash gave a puzzled frown at this statement, Fallon waved it aside. He studied the saloon owner: in contrast to Mace Coldfield, Nash did not bluster. Though his smile was friendly, it also showed a faint cynical quality, not especially bitter, but mellowed by experience. Nash appeared to be a man who had seen much of life and regarded the whole as a sort of comic entertainment. Somehow, Fallon felt an immediate liking for him.

"You're from the East, aren't you?" Fallon asked.

Nash nodded. "Born in Cambridge, Massachusetts. I attended Harvard, although that fact does not count for much out here."

"I've never been inside a school in my life."

Nash struck a match to a dark cigarette. "You're wrong there."

"How do you mean?"

Nash waved the cigarette in an all-encompassing circle. "The world, in a way, is a schoolroom. I left Harvard

40

dissatisfied. Books are a help, I'll admit, but the most important lessons are not taught in a classroom.''

"Then I guess I've learned a few," Fallon commented, the old bitterness in his voice.

"Prowess with a gun is one of them," Nash returned. "We need your kind of law in Longhorn, Mr. Fallon."

Fallon chuckled. "It's nice to hear somebody say that for a change. Most of the saloon owners haven't taken too kindly to the new rules."

"Especially Mace Coldfield, I'll wager," Nash replied, more mockery in his voice.

Fallon's eyebrows rose. "Yes. How did you know?"

Nash executed a relaxed shrug. "It fits, that's all."

"Fits? With what?"

"Let's say with the contemporary scene in the Washoe Basin."

Fallon debated with himself for a moment, then came to a decision. "Nash, maybe you can help me."

"For the favor you did my business, I'm glad to oblige if I can."

"What I need right now is a good, clear picture of what's going on in this town, and in the basin. I don't mean things as they are, out in the open. I mean behind the scenes, so to speak."

"Sheriff, my estimation of you rises every second. The lawmen we've had in here before have been totally unaware of the currents under the surface. Why are you interested in them?"

"Because I've got a feeling they might spell trouble."

Nash frowned thoughtfully. "And you're right. Well, where shall I begin?"

"How about these night riders?"

41

"Yes. You know of course that they struck again last night." Fallon nodded. "The popular belief is that they come from over the hills in the west. No, I ought to qualify that. People in the basin *say* they believe the riders come from over there. Actually, many people feel that Luke Mitchell and his Rocking L crew are the riders, but there is no definite proof of that, since the riders have never been caught, and never even given much opposition."

"That's what I don't understand," Fallon said. "Why don't the ranchers fight back?"

"Ah, Sheriff, there you've struck one of the unpleasant truths about mankind. People—ordinary people—need a leader. The ranchers lack unity, and they lack assurance. The night riders strike without warning, and get away with large herds of cattle. The ranchers never know who will be hit next. If it is true that Mitchell is the leader of the rustlers, he is safe as long as the ranchers refuse to act. They will not go after Mitchell directly, since they have no proof that he is running the raids. This basin is large. The ranchers are far apart. I'm afraid the only way the ranchers will be stirred to act is through the efforts of a determined leader. There is no such man among the ranchers themselves."

"I'm not much interested in getting into that scrap," Fallon said softly. "But I may not be able to help myself." Especially if Mitchell's men are really the night riders, he added to himself.

"It is believed that the night riders drive the cattle north, out of the basin at North Pass, to Halstead, which is another railhead."

"Sixty miles north," Fallon put in.

42

"Yes. Halstead at the present time has a reputation as a place where any man with five steers or more can sell them, no questions asked, regardless of the brand. That will probably change, in time, but at the moment, it provides someone with a very profitable living."

"But Mitchell may be behind the raids, you say?"

"Evidence points that way. His men know the cattle business, I'm told, but they're more than cowpunchers. They're gunslingers. I think I can recognize the professional look, and Mitchell's men have it."

"So I've noticed," murmured Fallon. Feeling that he had to trust someone if he wanted correct information, and recognizing that Nash was the first person in Longhorn who seemed to be in sympathy with his position, Fallon went ahead to outline briefly his suspicions about Coldfield. Through the recital, Nash studied his ciagrette with frowning concentration. When Fallon finished, Nash said:

"In other words, you think Coldfield came to you not merely because he was afraid business at the Crystal would be hurt, but for some other reason?"

"That's right."

"Interesting." Nash smiled thinly. "I'll be frank with you also, Sheriff. What I'm going to say is my own speculation, and I've never voiced it to any other man." Nash raised his eyes, cold now, and serious. "It has always struck me that Coldfield might have some connection with Mitchell, and if Mitchell is the leader of the night riders, Coldfield therefore might also be connected with the rustling. That's a dangerous assumption to make, especially with no proof. For absence of proof is what makes the ranchers afraid to act."

Fallon saw the wisdom of Nash's words. "Coldfield seems to have plenty of money. That big house, and his wife . . . well, I've wondered how many shots of rotgut it takes to pay for them."

Nash threw back his head and laughed. "Sheriff, I like you. We see things in the same light. I've asked myself that exact question. For India Coldfield—by the way, have you seen her?" Fallon nodded. "She's a handsome woman, but it's no secret that the cost of her upkeep is high. Coldfield imported her from Washington. She's a sort of showpiece for him, but she makes him pay the price. Drop down to the depot some evening. You'll see a trunk or two of dresses and other furnishings coming in from St. Louis on every train."

The sun had dropped low in the west, and shadows filled the corners of the office. Nash, a perceptive gleam in his eye, slowly blew twin plumes of smoke through his nostrils and crushed his cigarette under his heel. "A woman hounding a man for money can make him go to almost any lengths to get it. And Coldfield considers his wife his richest piece of property. He would never give her up."

Nash stood up. "I've rambled on long enough. That's about all I can tell you. Let me say again that I'm grateful for what you've done, and I'm not alone in feeling that way. If you want my appraisal of the situation in this basin, it's this: Coldfield is the man to watch out for. His wife, bleeding him for money, might provide a motive for his interest in stolen cattle. Therefore, he might be connected with Mitchell, who might be chief of the night riders." Nash's smile widened. "All of which might be wrong, and probably is."

Nash paused briefly, serious once more. "If Coldfield is the top man behind the raids, then he'll be your enemy, whether you provoke him directly or not. Because you've established your reputation. Your guns talk for you, and with more authority than we saw in three previous sheriffs, whose ineffectualness got them a piece of sod in the town cemetery. Even if you don't plan to make active war on the night riders, you're still a threat to them. A strong man is always dangerous, even if he is only passive, because you can never tell when he may get angered and start to fight. It would be good business for whoever is behind the trouble in the basin to stop intervention before it ever got started." Nash walked leisurely toward the door. "Forgive me, Sheriff. My vocabulary gets out of hand sometimes. I'm glad you're here in Longhorn, and if I can return the favor you did for me, I will."

Nash opened the door and stood framed in an oblong of light. All humor had been stripped from his face.

"A fuse burns in relative quiet," he said. "You may not realize it is burning until you hear the explosion. But the analogy's a good one to apply to things in Longhorn."

Nash paused. "I'd be careful."

He touched his hat and vanished through the door. Fallon stood a moment in the gathering shadows, feeling a sudden chill.

CHAPTER VII

FALLON ate his supper at a restaurant and began making his customary rounds. At midnight, with four boisterous punchers locked in the tank, he closed down his office and set off on foot for Mrs. Clay's boarding house. Once away from the main street, he found himself walking along dark, quiet streets. Most of the windows were dark too; here and there, however, a solitary lamp dappled the lawns beneath the trees.

He climbed the stairs of the boarding house to his room on the second floor, shed his vest, shirt and boots, and drew a tub of scalding water in the bathroom. He lay in the water for a little over an hour, relaxing. Then he put on a fresh shirt and boots, took a cigar and stepped out onto the second floor veranda. He left his gun belt, as usual, hanging on the post at the foot of the bed, but within easy reach of the porch through an open window. Sitting down and propping his feet on the veranda rail, he lit the cigar and tossed the match over into the alley below. Crickets harped in a bush. A dog barked sharply in the distance. Everyone else in the boarding house had gone to bed.

Fallon smoked his cigar down, threw it away and, supremely comfortable for a moment, with his feet still propped on the rail, closed his eyes. Sleep came swiftly.

In the second between the time he heard the noise and the time his eyes opened, thoughts chased through his mind with lightning speed. The bath had made him drowsier than usual; he had been a fool to leave his gun inside; this was the trouble he had expected.

He opened his eyes but did not move his head. Below, in the alley, he heard men walking, and farther back in the darkness, horses stamping restlessly. With a lithe movement, he bounded out of the chair and whirled around. Three shapes came at him from one end of the veranda: the dim glow from the lamp inside his room showed him black pits of eyes in the bleached feed sacks the men wore over their heads. They had climbed onto the veranda. Fallon whirled, searching the opposite direction for a means of escape, but two more of the phantom shapes were closing in on him from that quarter also.

He dove for the open window and his gun belt. A jolting knee caught him under the chin and slammed him to the side. Numbing pain shot along his nerves, but he scrambled to his feet and rocketed a fist at one of the night riders, sending the hooded man reeling backwards and sliding along the wall of the house.

Another of the attackers wrenched him around by the shoulder and smashed a fist against his jaw. Still another punched two hard blows home to Fallon's belly. A third kneed his groin with a harsh, quiet grunt of effort. Then came a rocking punch to Fallon's jaw that sent him stumbling backwards, unable to keep his balance. The back of his legs struck the veranda rail and he kept going. He seemed to be floating on a dark cloud for a second, and then his mind shouted that he was falling. He tried to twist in midair, and landed with a jarring crash on hands and knees, at the bottom of a ten-foot fall. He shook his head to clear it, and saw two more men advancing toward him through the gloom.

He jumped up, anger scorching him like a hot iron, and rushed the two night riders in the alley. He dodged aside as the first charged, stuck out his leg and tripped the man, chopping down on the man's neck as he fell. Then Fallon had only an instant in which to whirl about and send a punch at the second assailant. His opponent rolled with the blow and sent an equally smashing right against the side of Fallon's head.

Fallon charged again, whipping his right arm up with killing power. The man's jaw was more tender than Fallon's, for the sheriff's blow sent the other man backwards with a grunt of pain. Cat-like, Fallon slipped forward and hammered a half-dozen blows to the man's belly, then polished him off with another uppercut.

By that time, however, the men who had attacked him on the second floor porch were leaping down into the alley, striking earth with hard, smacking sounds. The man Fallon tripped came up behind him and grabbed him around the neck, so that he and Fallon fell in a tangled heap, scuffling in the dust. A thought burst on Fallon's mind like a blazing light:

They aren't using guns!

48

Now he knew what this attack was meant to be, and even as he wrestled with the night rider, who was reaching for his throat, he uttered a single mirthless syllable of laughter. The man caught Fallon's throat, his nails cutting deep into the flesh. Fallon choked momentarily in the thick dust rising from the scuffle, then worked his right arm free and smashed the elbow down onto the makeshift hood. The outlaw gasped and loosed his grip. Fallon reached for the man's holster and snaked the Colt free. The outlaw tried to fight back. Behind him, Fallon heard footsteps of the other night riders running toward him along the dark alley.

He leaped to his feet and silenced the man on the ground with a brutal boot heel in the man's face. Then he twisted, went into a crouch, and fired. The shot boomed and thundered in the alley. A red line spurted through the dark. But because of the hastiness of his shot, Fallon managed only to put a bullet in the right thigh of the first rider. The man went down while the other four raced past him. Lights were coming on in the boarding house now, but the fight had moved well to the rear of the house, and darkness still swallowed Fallon and the others almost completely.

Fallon tried to get off another shot.

The four night riders hit him all at once.

He went down in a confusion of harsh oaths and heavy grunts. He felt the muffling scrape of one of the rough feed sacks against his face. Boots slammed into his body. For a moment blows rained on his head in such profusion that he thought he must be fighting not four men but four hundred. Pain lanced along his nerves from a dozen different points. He kicked, flailed, struck out at any target, but they swarmed over him, striking viciously and hard. Warm blood spurted up into his mouth and smeared his lips. The dust stung his eyes. A heavy boot stomped on his stomach. His mind went red with pain. At last, he heard one of the attackers say something which resembled, " 'Nuff." The attackers backed off and conferred among themselves. Fallon lay for a minute, flat on his back in the dust, unable to move quickly. He had absorbed a terrific beating. His head rang, and it was impossible to recognize voices. With dogged determination, he rolled over on his side, tasting the blood and dirt in a thick mixture on his tongue. He rested a moment on all fours, still not completely conscious.

"What's going on out there?" demanded a feminine voice from the boarding house.

One of the night riders raised his gun and blasted away at the house. Window glass crashed. A lamp went out. Immediately, lamps in the windows of other curious boarders were extinguished. Fallon lurched to his feet and rushed for the five men. Only the man with his face stepped on and the one with the bullet hole in his thigh stayed out of the fight. They slunk along the alley into the darkness, and from the sounds that came to Fallon's ears, got the skittish horses ready.

Fallon plowed head first into the five, only to hear one of them laugh curtly. Hands pushed at Fallon, sending him backwards again. Two of the riders stepped around behind him, and held him erect. From behind a hood, one of the remaining three spoke.

"Take this for what it's worth, Sheriff. Leave Longhorn before you get killed." The man paused, his voice an indistinguishable blur. ''All right, you two. Leave him go and let's ride before we wake up the whole town.''

''We oughta . . .'' began one of the others who was holding Fallon.

''I said leave him go!'' Fallon had no trouble distinguishing the contempt in the leader's voice, however. ''He's whipped.''

With a push to help him, Fallon fell forward again and smashed into the dust. The night riders walked off down the alley, heading for their horses.

Get up, Fallon thought in angry fury. *Get up!*

He stumbled to his feet once more, and wondered what he could use for a weapon. His eye lit on the fallen Colt he had dropped earlier; the barrel gleamed faintly in the distant glow from the street. He scooped it up and started forward at a run, toward the men just mounting up farther back in the darkness.

''Look out there!'' one of them shouted in warning.

Fallon stopped and squeezed the trigger, sure of his aim. One of the riders screamed and clutched his belly. His horse reared, pawing the air, screaming louder. The other horses spooked and the riders fought for control. ''Grab him!'' one of them shouted, as the dead man started to pitch from his saddle. He was caught, however, and dragged off his mount onto another horse. The leader's horse broke into a run down the alley toward Fallon, and the others followed. Fallon saw pistols coming free now. The night riders had been driven to a killing rage.

For a moment Fallon stood rooted, unable to move. The band of horsemen plunged toward him along the alley like demons out of hell, hoods flapping as they rode. Colts came up. The hoofbeat roar rose to an ear-shattering thunder. Fallon fired another shot, missed, and flung himself toward the shrubbery at the edge of the boarding house lawn. He struck the bushes and kept rolling, clawing his way through the tangle of branches. The riders swept past. Guns flamed and roared. Bullets sang around Fallon's head like angry bees, and struck the ground with vicious, smacking sounds. Then the riders swept on, out into the street and away. The hoofbeats died gradually. The noise of the crickets rasping in the shrubbery could again be heard.

CHAPTER VIII

FALLON was up, dressed and in the saddle at false dawn. He rode out of Longhorn at a gallop, heading into the Washoe Basin, toward the Wheeler ranch.

The Box W spread owned by Asa Wheeler was situated some twelve miles out of Longhorn. Fallon passed a few other ranches as he rode; he caught sight here and there of a herd bedded down and weary cowpokes standing guard against the threat of a raid. But usually only one, or at the most two guards watched over each herd; hardly enough protection against the night riders.

Fallon rode on, drinking deep of the winy morning air. The sky began to gray in the east. Far in the distance toward the western hills, a campfire flickered in the peaceful coolness just before dawn. The vast shadowy reaches of the basin, with land and hills blurring together in a blue-gray haze of half-light, seemed to be drowsing in eternal peace. A false peace really, Fallon thought to himself. Men everywhere broke in on nature's quiet and they would, in time, make blood run on the earth of the Washoe Basin. . . .

A crew of fence riders, half a mile distant, hallooed as they loped by, a ghostly legion. At last, however, the eastern foothills began to drip molten light from their summits and the cool haze began to part. The sun was just in sight as Fallon reined in the Box W yard. Punchers were coming from the bunkhouse and ambling toward their mounts in the corral. A couple of them nodded to Fallon in a reserved way. Fallon strode to the porch of the rambling frame ranch house.

"Is Wheeler inside?" he asked of the boy leaning indolently against a post that supported the porch roof.

"Guess so," the boy replied. "See for yourself, why don't you?"

Fallon shot the boy a hard glance, which the boy ignored as he stared blandly out into the ranch yard. Fallon opened the door and stepped into the hall. Aromas of fried eggs, flapjacks and coffee drifted to his nostrils.

"Somebody asking for me?" came Asa Wheeler's voice from the dining room. The rancher peered into the hall. "Oh, hello there, Sheriff. Come on in and light down. Have a cup of coffee?" Fallon accepted with pleasure, dropping into a chair and draining half a cup of the steaming black brew. Wheeler resumed his seat, wiped his mouth with his shirt sleeve and, wrinkling up his grizzled brows, said:

"Mighty early for you to be riding out this way, isn't it?"

"I've got something important to talk over with you."

"Important? Well . . . say!" Wheeler leaned forward

across the table, scrutinizing the bruises and clotted cuts on Fallon's cheeks, jaw and forehead. "What happened to your face? Looks like you got stomped on by a loco steer."

"By a small herd of 'em," Fallon replied sardonically. "The night riders paid me a visit last night. They worked me over pretty thoroughly, and told me that if I wanted to stay alive, I should get out of Longhorn and forget about being a lawman."

Wheeler appeared startled. "Now why in thunderation should they pick on you? You haven't gone after them."

"But I imagine they figured I would, sooner or later."

Wheeler scratched his jaw. "Yep, that makes sense, I suppose. Those varmints with sacks over their heads may look sort o' comic, but believe me, they've got me plenty worried. So far they haven't touched any Box W stock —I guess because I've got the largest spread in the Washoe—but I get the feeling now and then that they won't leave my herd alone much longer."

Fallon sat forward, slamming his fist lightly on the dining table. The sugar bowl rattled. "Then why don't you and the other ranchers band together and fight them?"

Wheeler hesitated, disturbed and even slightly embarrassed. "Sheriff, there's no really good reason, I reckon, except that humans are always slow to fight back. Why, when the railroad first came into Longhorn, plenty of folks figured that somebody might get hurt where the tracks cross Peach Street—that's on the edge of town, as you come in. There are plenty of houses on that street, and people cross the tracks all the time. Six months ago, the little Skinner boy got killed by a train at that crossing, and folks in Longhorn finally decided it was time to take action. So they hired old Pop Bates to be a watchman at the crossing, when he's sober.'' Wheeler sighed loudly and lifted one hand. ''It takes read bad trouble to make folks realize they've waited too long already to take action. I'm no better'n the rest.''

''That still doesn't explain why the ranchers let the night riders rustle their stock,'' Fallon countered. ''Does it?''

Wheeler pondered. ''Most of the ranchers in this basin are peaceful men with families. The night riders haven't killed anybody yet in their raids, and maybe all of us out here are just a little bit scared to start gunplay. Oh, we have guards on the herds at night, a man or two, but the riders don't hit too often, and . . .'' Wheeler's words faded off dispiritedly. He stared at his empty coffee cup. ''What I'm saying all of a sudden sounds mighty feeble. I guess humans are humans, and as poor an excuse as that is, it's all us ranchers have got.''

''In other words,'' Fallon spoke softly, ''the night riders bleed you dry, little by little, and you don't fight back. If they hit you all at once, say—if they rustled two or three thousand head and killed half a dozen men, you'd fight.''

''Yes, we would.''

''But don't you see,'' Fallon insisted, ''that if you let them run off the little herds, pretty soon they *will* be making bigger raids? It's only a question of time.''

''I never quite looked at it that way,'' Wheeler said, musing.

''Have any of the night riders ever been killed during the raids?''

"No," Wheeler said thoughtfully, "not that I recollect. The guards usually fire a couple of shots, but the riders swarm all over 'em and knock 'em senseless, then just leave them. . . ."

"I killed one of the night riders last night," Fallon told him. "I'm almost positive of it. And I wounded another."

Wheeler emitted a low whistle. "Boy, they will be after you for fair now!"

Fallon's gray-blue eyes remained hard, even cold. "But I'm not running. I don't like being threatened like that, and I aim to make the night riders know it."

"I think I'm beginnin' to get the drift . . ." Wheeler told him.

"Let's organize the ranchers and stamp out this trouble before it goes any further!" Fallon said vehemently. "Don't just sit on your backsides, waiting for the rustlers to take every head of beef you've got. Show some resistance. A few men may get hurt, but you'll save yourselves a lot more grief in the long run. Doesn't that sound sensible?"

"Yep," Wheeler replied. He nodded emphatically. "Yep, it surely does. It sounds so sensible that I'm plumb ashamed I haven't thought of it myself, long before this."

Fallon, realizing that at last he had penetrated beneath the apathy of Asa Wheeler, felt a grim triumph. If Wheeler could help in organizing the other ranchers, it might not be long before Fallon had others of the marauding band under his gun. The death's head smile fleeted across his face once more as he thought of this.

Wheeler asked, "Have you got a plan, Sheriff?"

"The first step is to call a meeting of the ranchers, and

I'll tell them what I told you. You swing plenty of influence in the basin. . . ."

"Well, I don't know . . ." Wheeler began.

"No sense being modest, Wheeler. It's true. If you back this play, I think the other ranchers will join in right away. How would next Monday night be for the meeting? Is that too soon?"

Wheeler stood up, and Fallon thought he saw a new firmness in the set of the grizzled rancher's jaw. "Tonight wouldn't be soon enough, but it'll take till Monday to get all the other owners in the basin rounded up. I'll send my riders around to the other spreads. Monday night, about eight o'clock?"

Fallon rose also. "Fine. I guess I can be riding, then."

Wheeler accompanied Fallon to the porch. The sun had risen completely now, flooding the yard with warm golden light. A brisk, cool breeze came in from the northwest. Wheeler studied Fallon a moment with a speculative look. "You're mighty interested in seeing the night riders stopped, aren't you, Sheriff?"

"I am, after what happened last night."

"If this works out, you'll be doing me and the other owners a big favor."

Fallon said nothing. *Better not antagonize him.* But what Fallon really thought was: *I don't do favors for anybody. This is personal.* Wheeler said, "Before I forget it, let me give you an invite to the dance Saturday night."

"Dance?"

"We hold 'em once a month, at the Social Hall in town."

"That's a little out of my line."

"Hell's fire, Sheriff, a man can't stay cooped up by

himself all the time. You need to loosen up a little. You're officially invited now, so we'll be looking for you there.''

Fallon started to reply when he noticed Piney Woods coming toward the porch with a grin on his face. The little puncher walked eagerly, fast, moving his crippled leg as best he could. Wheeler said, ''Oh-oh. You won't get away for a while now. All Piney can talk about is the way you helped him out in the Crystal. I'm mighty grateful too, by the way. And he thinks you're practically Gawd-on-earth. . . .''

Fallon shifted uncomfortably. The look of open adulation in Piney's eyes as he came across the yard made Fallon writhe inwardly. ''Greetin's, Mr. Fallon!'' Piney exclaimed as he arrived at the porch steps. ''I thought it was you. Come out to look the spread over?''

''Not exactly,'' Fallon returned.

''Want me to show you around?''

''Well . . .''

Fortunately, one of the other hands rode into the yard at that moment and asked Asa Wheeler to come take a look at one of the new-born calves. Wheeler excused himself, which gave Fallon a moment to think, but the respite was temporary. Fallon could think of no words to speak to the little puncher that would not be a direct insult. Piney showed no inclination to move from his position at the foot of the porch steps. Fallon contemplated telling him simply to get out of the way and quit pestering him.

Instead, he drew a deep breath and said, ''Piney, let's get something straight between us.''

Baffled, the little puncher replied, ''Why, sure, Mr. Fallon. Is anything wrong?''

''No, nothing's wrong, exactly.'' Fallon groped for

words. "It's just that I don't like being set up as some sort of little tin god. Get it out of your head that I did something special for you. I would have done the same for anyone else."

If Fallon had expected to see self-pity on Piney's face, he had expected the wrong emotion, for Piney threw back his tiny shoulders and raised his diminutive chin in such a show of stiff pride that Fallon felt a little embarrassed.

"I told you outside the Crystal that I fought my own battles, Mr. Fallon. That still goes. I don't need pity from anybody, and I don't expect it. I hold my own. I'm still grateful, though. You saved my life. I won't forget it. If it goes against your grain . . . well, I'm sorry, that's all."

Fallon stared at the small puncher, wondering what drove him to this fantastic loyalty.

Abruptly, he grew conscious of another pair of eyes on him, and he turned to the right. Down at the end of the porch stood Kate Wheeler, a milk pail in her hand. Evidently she had listened to the whole conversation, for she treated Fallon to a stony stare, turned on her heel and disappeared around the corner of the house.

Fallon stepped off the porch, and Piney shuffled backwards out of the way. "I've got to be riding, Piney," Fallon said tersely.

As Fallon headed for his horse, a pair of shots split the morning quiet, smacking up spurts of dust a foot away from his boots. Instantly, experiencing the old reaction, Fallon went into a slight crouch and swept his Colt free of leather. Two more shots sounded to the left, and Fallon heard the crash of glass being shattered. Fallon threw a glance at Piney that said, What's going on?

Piney started in the direction of the shots at an awkward run. "That fool Chip again . . ." he cried.

Fallon ran after him, Colt at the ready. He rounded the corner of the house and pulled up short. On the other side of the corral rail, pistol raised, stood the boy Fallon had met on the porch when he first arrived. Fallon figured his age to be nineteen or thereabouts; thin, he had pale blue eyes, black hair and a surly expression. His clothes appeared a bit too dudish for the average ranch hand, especially the black vest with its design of red and white beads, and the flowing gray silk bandana knotted carelessly around his throat.

Along the top rail of the corral stood three empty whisky bottles in a row. Fragments of broken glass glittered in the sun on the ground just below.

Fallon and Piney faced the boy with the bottles on the fence directly between them. The boy pulled the trigger of the gun again, a bottle shattered, glass rained on the ground, and the bullet *zzzed* by Fallon's ear at too close range. Shoving his own Colt savagely into the holster, Fallon raced forward, vaulted the corral rail and wrenched the gun from the boy's hand. The boy threw his fist back as if to hit Fallon, but the deadly *snick-snick* of the cocking gun in the sheriff's hand stopped him.

"You're pretty careless with this iron, youngster," Fallon said coldly.

"Don't call me 'youngster,' " the youth shot back.

"You don't deserve to be called anything else until you learn that a gun's not to be played with."

The boy stood in a swaggering pose, openly defiant. "Let me have that gun back."

"I ought to let you have the butt of it in your teeth."

"Listen." The youth jabbed out an index finger. "I know you're Reb Fallon, and that you're a short trigger artist, but that doesn't mean a thing to me."

"Try this stunt in town and you'll spend a while behind bars," retorted Fallon. He knew he could not take on this youth in a fist fight, because he outmatched the boy both in weight and experience. To start gunplay would result in nothing less than the boy's murder. But Fallon burned with wrath at the sight of this cocky kid, wearing fancy clothes, supremely confident that he was master of the world.

As Fallon stared at the youth, a horse pounded up to the corral entrance and Asa Wheeler leaped off. He yanked the gate open and came striding toward Piney, Fallon and the boy. "What's going on here?" he demanded. "I heard shots. . . . Chip, what in blazes have you been up to?"

"Nothin'," Chip replied, but he averted his eyes quickly from Fallon. "I was only doing a little target practice. What's the harm in that?"

"The harm is that somebody could of got killed!" Piney explained. Briefly, he told Wheeler what had happened. The cattleman's expression grew thunderous.

"Sheriff," Wheeler said, "this is my nephew, Chip Wheeler. After what I've just heard, I'm sorry that he's kin of mine."

"Aw, Uncle Asa . . ." began Chip Wheeler in a whining tone.

"Don't you 'Uncle Asa' me! I've had enough of your helling. . . ."

"I'm not going to stand here and listen to this," Chip said threateningly.

"Don't sass me, Chip," Wheeler warned. "I can still take a whip to you. You're not that big."

Chip seemed temporarily cowed. Fallon handed his gun to the boy with a savage shove which thrust the butt forward so that it gouged Chip's belly. The youth's pale blue eyes flamed with anger. But the words of his uncle had evidently tamed him a little. "Next time," Fallon said with ice in his tone, "you might get shot at right back. And you'd deserve it."

"Agh!" Chip uttered the contemptuous sound under his breath. He turned quickly and left the corral. In the ranch yard, he mounted, and with a curse, dug his spurs savagely into his animal's side. The horse plunged out of the yard in a gallop. Chip's gray silk bandana streamed in the wind behind him as he vanished up the road to Longhorn.

CHAPTER IX

ALTHOUGH Fallon dismissed the idea of going to the dance as soon as Asa Wheeler brought it up, the sheriff found himself restless when Saturday night finally arrived. As he ate his dinner in the restaurant, he told himself that his presence at the affair would be a sort of admission of defeat. But Longhorn seemed especially quiet as he made his rounds at seven o'clock, and as he passed the Social Hall, he paused on the opposite side of the street to watch several buggies arrive, filled with eager, laughing celebrants. Light poured from the windows of the frame building, and he could hear the scrape-screech of fiddles being tuned up. The sight of people gathered together instilled in him a biting loneliness which all of his coldly realistic thoughts could not put down. With an exclamation of disgust at his own behavior, he turned sharply away and savagely puffed a cigar alight as he walked.

By eight-thirty, however, he gave in to his strong inner feelings.

Returning to Mrs. Clay's, he drew a quick bath and changed into his suit. He ran a comb through his sandy hair and clipped a few stray hairs from his mustaches. Then he walked back to the Social Hall, following the lure of fiddle music and laughing voices drifting through the darkness. As he turned in at the brightly lighted doorway, he said to himself, *"You're as skittish as a young colt trying its legs. You hope Kate Wheeler will be here."* And though he disliked admitting it even to himself, this was true.

"Evening, Sheriff!" exclaimed the man on duty at the door, with surprise.

"Ah . . . evening," Fallon said a trifle awkwardly. The stiff shirt collar chafed his neck, and he was beginning to feel warm.

"Come right on in," the man grinned. "Better let me check your gun belt for you, though. It's kind of unhandy to dance with an iron on your hip."

Fallon slid his gun across the counter and stepped into the hall proper. Some three dozen couples, young and old alike, circled the dance floor to the strains of a waltz played by a trio of musicians. To the left stood a table heaped with pastries and a punch bowl. To his right, a pair of open doors led outside. By one of these Chip Wheeler stood, attired in a black suit with a loud gray stripe. The youth, talking to an attractive young girl, caught sight of Fallon and their eyes locked momentarily. Chip's expression displayed open contempt. He said something humorous to the girl, threw his curly-haired head back, laughed and, bending low to whisper in the blushing girl's ear, directed her firmly out through a door into the darkness.

Fallon stood frowning for a moment. There could be no denying the fact that he had made still one more enemy in the person of Chip Wheeler.

Feeling that people were staring at him, Fallon threaded his way through the crowd toward the punch bowl. Though he expected a watery fruit-flavored concoction, he found that the cut glass cup of liquid handed to him was liberally laced with liquor, and his stomach warmed pleasantly. He was about to select a slice of cake when the dance ended, applause spattered briefly, and someone touched his arm.

It was difficult to turn around smoothly and calmly when a touch on the arm usually meant an enemy behind, but he managed it. Startled, he came face to face with India Coldfield.

"You're Fallon, aren't you?" she inquired, though her black eyes said she already knew.

"That's correct."

"I'm India Coldfield."

"I know."

"Do you?" The delicate black eyebrows arched, broken bird wings against the pale cream sky of the woman's forehead. An expensive scent, mixed with another odor Fallon could not quite place, arose from her throat and shoulders. "I'm flattered." She wore a gown of black silk, cut a good bit lower than the gowns worn by the other women at the dance. India Coldfield tapped a black lace fan lightly against one palm. "I felt it my civic duty to make the acquaintance of the man who is finally bringing law and order to Longhorn." Though a smile curved the woman's lips, light mockery danced in her tone.

"Would you care for some punch?" Fallon asked a bit stiffly.

"No, thank you. The brew in that bowl isn't quite strong enough to suit my taste. Would I be too forward if I asked you to dance with me?"

Fallon had caught sight of Mace Coldfield standing by himself along the rear wall, smoking. It was evident from Coldfield's solitary vigil, as well as from the way certain other ladies in the vicinity looked at India Coldfield, that the saloon keeper and his wife were not exactly welcome at the gathering. Coldfield appeared to be looking in the other direction when Fallon saw him.

"How does your husband act when you dance with another man?" Fallon asked.

"Mace?" She laughed, but it had a harsh sound. "He is the jealous type, but I'm sure you can handle yourself well." She raised her arms in invitation as the fiddles took up another waltz tune. "Don't be afraid, Mr. Fallon," she purred mockingly.

Fallon swept her out onto the dance floor. He had trouble for a moment remembering how this dance went, but before long he had recalled the step and could concentrate his attention on the woman in his arms.

"You dance well, Mr. Fallon," she said.

He shook his head. "That can't be true. I haven't danced for years."

"Perhaps it's the way you hold me, then. Your hands are strong. They make a woman feel secure."

Fallon deftly changed the subject. "I didn't expect to see the reigning belle of Longhorn here. These people are mostly ranchers."

"And a dull, unimaginative lot. I'll agree." She sighed. "I'd give my soul to see the Potomac again, or ride down Pennsylvania Avenue. I hate this town. You at least make this dance tolerable. Mace wouldn't bring me, but I insisted. Lord knows there's little enough excitement in this village." The last word seethed with contempt.

"It's my job to see that things don't get too exciting," he told her.

Her eyelids veiled the blackness of her gaze for a moment. So that he could barely hear, she whispered, "I meant a different sort of excitement." Her hand, in his, constricted more tightly for a moment. "Longhorn could be a very pleasant place, Mr. Fallon, provided you keep your health."

His spine prickled. "Is that supposed to mean something special?"

"Decide for yourself." Though she spoke lightly, her words concealed an undertone of warning. "A man who goes looking for trouble, regardless of where he may be, is automatically reducing his own chances for a long life. The longer a man lives, the longer he may enjoy himself."

Fallon framed a reply, but had no opportunity to deliver it. The music came to a halt, and India excused herself. She swept regally across the floor and linked her arm with her husband's, but she still had a lingering, suggestive gaze for Fallon which Coldfield appeared to ignore. The saloon owner guided his wife toward the entrance with obvious impatience.

Fallon, searching the throng for Kate Wheeler, did not locate her. He returned to the table, took up his punch cup from where he had left it, drained it and got a refill immediately. Two dances went by while Fallon made conversation with Oscar Hawkins, the bald, good-humored rancher. Finally Fallon spotted Kate Wheeler coming in through one of the side doors on the arm of a young cowhand.

Fallon set down his cup. "Excuse me, Mr. Hawkins," he said, though he was already a foot away from the rancher, walking rapidly through the crowd.

"Sure, Sheriff, sure. . . ." Hawkins' voice drifted behind him with a knowing chuckle.

For some reason, Kate Wheeler's face stood out among the others in the crowd like a shining light. Her coppery hair glowed softly, and her gray eyes sparkled as she conversed with the cowhand. Though her dress, of red and green checks, was obviously home-sewn, and considerably less modish than the one India Coldfield had worn, it still showed her figure to wonderful advantage. Fallon was conscious of an unreasonable lump in his throat as he approached her.

"Miss Wheeler. . . ."

"Oh, good evening, Mr. Fallon." She smiled warmly, seemed to remember who he was and regret the smile a second later. She performed introductions, but Fallon shook the puncher's hand mechanically and did not even hear his name.

"I wondered if I could have the next dance," Fallon asked.

Kate hesitated, then said, "Of course. Excuse me, Jack."

The music began. As they moved out onto the floor, he was conscious of a number of things: the clean, wind-fresh scent of her skin and hair; the closeness of her womanly figure, even though she danced with a good deal more propriety than India Coldfield; and the sudden leaden clumsiness of his own feet. Twice in the space of their first minute together, he made awkward apologies for stepping on her toes.

Could he be mistaken? Was that a warming spark of friendliness he saw in her eyes? The music, the nearness of her affected him strangely. Watch out! his mind warned.

"I do owe you a debt of gratitude," she told him.

"Oh?" Fallon grinned easily. "My stock's going up."

She colored slightly. "I said once before I had nothing personal against you. I wanted to thank you for the way you took Chip's gun away from him the other day."

Fallon looked at her closely. "I've seen too many kids like him along the frontier. A gun is a tool, not something to show off with. If a youngster makes a practice of showing off with his iron, one day he'll meet someone who can show off a little faster. And there'll be one more slow draw victim in the cemetery." He grinned. "But that's a pretty gloomy topic to bring up on a night like this. Tell me, do you really dislike me so much?"

Averting her eyes, the girl replied with a trace of hesitancy, "I dislike what you stand for. Perhaps I wish I didn't have to." Briskly, controlling her emotions, she raised her eyes squarely to his again. "I don't want cousin Chip to get into trouble. I believe in him. I think he's a good boy. Oh, he may be a bit wild, but he'll tame down eventually. He hates the Washoe Basin, and the whole West, in fact—my uncle, his father, raised Chip in Chicago, and naturally the boy's used to quite a different life. But I have faith in Chip," she said fervently. "Dad thinks there's little hope for him. I disagree. I know Chip spends too much of his time in saloons when he should be working, but he's young and . . ."

"Whoa!" Fallon said pleasantly. "You don't have to justify the lad to me."

"Forgive me." She laughed.

Fallon found speech difficult. "Miss Wheeler . . . Kate . . ." she did not seem to mind the use of her first name . . . "I'd like to ask you something else."

"What is it?"

"Could we call a truce?"

"Truce?"

"What I mean to say is . . . I'd like to have you on my side."

She studied him as they moved in time to the music. The voices of the other couples around them buzzed away in the distance. There was no one else in the entire room with Fallon except this copper-haired girl.

"I don't understand why you ask such a thing," Kate replied.

"Don't you?"

She raised her gray eyes, and for the first time he felt he had broken through her wall of reserve. In her eyes shone an emotion that seemed to be forcing itself into the open. "Of course I understand," she told him softly. "But . . ."

"Yes?"

"We can't escape the way things are," she said a little desperately. "I can't escape the way I feel."

"About what, for instance?"

71

"Well, take Piney Woods."

"What about him?"

"You saved his life. He worships you for it. He'd do anything in the world for you."

"I doubt that," Fallon replied wryly.

"Nevertheless it's true. And he simply can't understand why you won't accept him as a friend. I can't either. I'd like to, Reb . . . no, I simply won't call you by that name."

"My real name is Eli."

"All right; Eli it is. Women are trained to speak their minds here. No polite eastern hinting. I want to like you. But I can't because I don't understand you. Why, for instance, are you helping Dad organize against the night riders? I think it's a fine idea—if you can do it without too much bloodshed." Fallon, about to reply, kept his peace. "But why are you doing it? I won't believe it's because you want to see justice done. Nor will I believe you're doing it because it's part of your job. You could ignore the night riders completely for months, and concentrate on your duties here in town, and no one would blame you."

"Did you hear about the beating the night riders gave me?"

"Yes."

"I intend to pay them back."

"It's all for yourself, then? You don't care about helping anyone else, like you could help Piney by being his friend?"

"All for myself," Fallon returned. "I told you when we first met that you wouldn't like the way my mind works."

"But why do you feel that way?" she demanded passionately.

"Because I can't believe that people are worth helping. People are selfish. In this world it's every man for himself, dog eat dog. I may be no better than the rest, but I'm no worse, either."

With puzzlement, not anger, she gave her head a vigorous shake. "I wish I could understand why you feel . . ."

Almost without their knowing it, the music came to a halt. They clapped, but disinterestedly. Fallon felt that it was suddenly very necessary to tell this girl about himself, in the hope that she alone, of all the women he had ever met, would understand. He took her elbow gently. "Would you really like to know why I feel the way I do?" She nodded. "Come outside with me then."

They walked through one of the side doors, out under the trees. The leaves rustled softly up above, and the night wind set tiny tendrils of her hair a-dancing. As they stood in semi-darkness Fallon spoke, calmly, not with self-pity, but revealing the facts.

He told her of his father, a seaman—"One bad Irishman out of all the good ones"—who had landed one year in Salem, Massachusetts, and wooed the daughter of a leading family. The marriage had come after an elopement. Sean Fallon had the sea-smell over him and a silver sound to his talk, and the devil of adventure in his blue eyes. Elizabeth Preston had never known a life outside of the sedate drawing rooms of New England, where ancestors in gold frames looked down with the stern eye of tradition. The child's name—Eli, with a Yankee sound, combined with Fallon, was itself symbolic of the union of two ways of life that could never endure as one. Elizabeth Fallon died in a cheap rooming house in Philadelphia, three days after her son was born.

Sean Fallon gave up the sea and turned to his only other talent: gambling. His son grew up in the brawling sin-pit that was Natchez-Under-the-Hill; his playthings were a pair of dice or a deck of cards. Sean Fallon, a broken man, sat red-faced under the lamps, drinking more heavily, losing more frequently, unwilling to make a try at a different life. One night there was an argument with a riverman, and Sean Fallon, his red face fuddled, could not get his derringer free of his vest pocket in time. What little soul he had left fled through the dark slash in his throat.

"I was on my own when I was ten," Fallon told Kate Wheeler. "I worked on the river boats, and everywhere I went, I saw people grabbing, cheating, scheming, to get something at the expense of another person."

While the night wind rustled the trees, Fallon told Kate Wheeler about Marie, the New Orleans woman who had whispered that she loved him, all the while scheming for a gown that would eventually win her another husband.

"When the War Between the States came," Fallon continued, "I enlisted. I learned how to handle a gun in the army, and how to handle it well. I thought I might find things different in the army. I didn't. One time there was a Yankee charge, and the blue boys were coming through our line. I saw one of them throw up a rifle to shoot my commanding officer, a captain. The captain reached out and grabbed an enlisted man next to him and used him for a shield. The enlisted man took the bullet in the skull; the captain turned and ran. Nothing had changed. Nothing has changed now.

"After the war, I got tired of being able to do nothing but lift packing cases on a dock all day, or drive a brewery wagon, so I drifted out here. I had no trade, I had no education. All I had was a little talent with a pistol . . . so I practiced, and got better. The only way I could get anything at all out of life was to wear a faster gun than the next man. The rest," Fallon shrugged, "you know. I'm a professional lawman. I do it because it pays."

Kate stood silent, overwhelmed. Then she spoke with quiet earnestness. "But all people aren't selfish. I know that's hard to believe, from all the things you've seen, but it's true! There are good things in life . . . more good things than the money you get for wearing a badge."

Fallon stared off into the darkness. "I wish I could believe it. I can't."

But strangely, he found himself desperately wanting to.

He turned to look once more at Kate Wheeler. A hopeless, defeated quality had come into her expression. Fallon cursed himself. He had spoiled things, broken the slender bond of understanding between them.

"I'm wishing something too," she said softly. She stood very close to him now, her face upraised, a white glow in the night. "I'm wishing that I knew how to change your thinking. But I don't. And two people have to think alike . . . I mean basically. . . ." She sobbed. "Oh, I don't know what I'm saying!" Distraught, she whirled around and ran quickly toward the lighted door of the Social Hall. Fallon did not follow her. The confused, agonized throb of her words lingered in the air long after she had gone.

CHAPTER X

THE night riders struck again that same night.

Almost at the exact moment in which Fallon was striding away from the Social Hall, the hooded rustlers swept down on the herd of a ranch near the edge of the basin. The ranch belonged to a man named Branneman. Three hundred odd head were run off. Three of Branneman's punchers were wounded, and a man called Forrester, the top hand, was shot to death. The news caused a considerable stir in Longhorn next day, amid the drowsy whispers of carriage wheels rolling to church through the sun-drenched dust. As Fallon sat in his office, cleaning and oiling his Colt, and listening to the distant peal of a church bell in the still morning air, he felt that the new raid would help his cause at the meeting the following night. As usual, the night riders had left no clues to their identity. If they had suffered casualties, the wounded had been carefully helped away from the scene of the fight. That situation, Fallon hoped, would soon be remedied.

As the church bell pealed and families from all over the basin gathered for the morning services, Fallon sat alone in the stuffy heat of his office, methodically cleaning his gun.

CHAPTER XI

TOWARD eight, on Monday evening, Fallon rode slowly in the direction of the Box W. A cool, bracing wind whipped out of the northwest, and he bent forward slightly in the saddle, meeting the brunt of the wind head on. He rode into the yard, tied his horse next to several others, each bearing a different brand, and greeted Piney Woods with a good feeling he could not altogether explain.

"Evening, Piney."

"Howdy, Mr. Fallon. You're right on time. Mr. Wheeler told me you had something important on your mind to say tonight." The bantam-sized cowhand seemed deliberately reserved.

"Right."

"Well, most of the ranchers are inside, so we might as well go on in. I—oh, here come the last two now. Hawkins and Field."

Fallon turned to see the short, bald Oscar Hawkins and another cattleman gallop into the yard. They tied their mounts beside the other horses and buggies which were assembled before the ranch house. Hawkins and his companion, a tall, spare rancher with a gingery mustache and a severe countenance, stepped up on the porch. Hawkins gave his usual jovial greeting, but Field was cool.

"I think you ought to know that I came here only because Asa Wheeler asked me to," Field informed Fallon. "I have a good idea of what this meeting is all about, and I believe in speaking my mind."

"So do I," Fallon replied, again measuring his opposition.

"You'll have your chance," Lucius Field said in a chilly tone. "I'm a peaceable man. I don't believe in hasty action." Decisively, Field bit off the end of a cigar, spat it and marched into the house. Hawkins followed, then Piney, and Fallon last. Fallon knew that Lucius Field would play an important part in the success or failure of his scheme, even though Field was a bit too old to do much actual fighting. Fallon had heard of Field; he owned one of the larger spreads in the Washoe Basin, was reputed to be highly conservative, and was also highly respected, not only for his savvy of the cattle business, but for the fact that somehow he had once studied two years at an eastern university.

Fallon and the others passed through the front hall. Asa Wheeler appeared from the parlor, and pumped Field's hand vigorously. "Good to see you, Lucius. Glad you could make it. Greetings, Sheriff. Come on in and light down. Looks like we have the whole crowd."

Stepping into the parlor, Fallon was instantly aware of a dozen pairs of eyes studying him. The ranchers ceased talking among themselves and settled forward on the edge of their chairs, awaiting what would happen next. Swiftly Fallon scrutinized the ring of faces. He saw uneasiness on one face, suspicion on another, pure disinterestedness on a third. He saw also sarcastic defiance, though it was subdued, on the face of Chip Wheeler, who lounged indolently on a sofa, smoking a brown cigarette.

"Chip, get your lazy hind end off there and make room for Lucius," Wheerer ordered. A few self-conscious chuckles sounded through the room. Chip's eyes blazed, but he held himself in check, and retired to lean against the fireplace. Lucius Field settled himself in the center of the group, clearly a sort of reigning patriarch, aloof, who balanced Asa Wheeler's down to earth leadership. Fallon, offered a chair, preferred to stand. His palms felt sweaty.

He wondered where Kate was.

Wheeler cleared his throat, scratched his chin and began: "Men, I guess I owe you a word or two of explanation for callin' this meeting. The sheriff here has something he wants to say to all of you. I've asked all of my boys who aren't out riding night herd to listen, too, because I think what the sheriff is going to tell us is something that needs to be thought over—and seriously—by every single man in this room who plans to keep on livin' in the Washoe Basin." Wheeler threw a glance at Lucius Field, who sat with crossed legs, unimpressed. "It's no secret," Wheeler continued, "that those night riders have been causing us trouble. . . ."

"But not serious trouble," Lucius Field cut in. "Not serious enough to warrant the formation of a vigilante group, if that's the idea, Asa."

"This is not Mr. Wheeler's idea," Fallon said sharply.

"I'll take the responsibility, since it appears that there may be some opposition." The barb angered Field, and Fallon immediately chalked it up as a tactical error.

A small man with pale blue eyes—Branneman, whose spread had been hit Saturday night—spoke up. "I'd call having my top hand shot serious trouble, Lucius. It's serious enough when a man like Forrester, my top hand, has got a wife and a couple of kids, and they don't know how they're going to live now that Forrester's dead."

A murmur of assent ran round the room.

Field harrumphed faintly, but his flinty gaze moderated a little. He made no comment.

"Maybe I'd better do my own explaining," Fallon said to Wheeler. Wheeler agreed.

Fallon began in a calm, persuasive voice, sketching the picture as he had done for Wheeler the previous week. Letting the night riders get away with small raids now would only increase their confidence and open the way for larger, bolder strikes in the future. As Fallon spoke, his voice gathered power, drawing on the anger that had been kindled when the night riders struck at him. Lamplight flickered behind painted glass bowls, and Fallon watched the eyes of the ranchers as they exchanged glances. Suspicion changed to agreement. Disinterestedness became fervor. Even Lucius Field appeared to lose himself in thoughtful speculation.

"So it's time to fight them!" Fallon concluded. "Before there's nothing left in the Washoe but the bones of the dead steers the rustlers couldn't drive off!"

"We shouldn't go into this hastily, though," Field hedged.

Fallon knew he had to drive his attack home. "Mr.

81

Field, if you walked into Wheeler's house here and stole ten dollars from a desk drawer, and Wheeler saw you and did nothing, didn't even try to stop you, what would you do?''

Field smiled icily. ''Sheriff, I'm not so stubborn that I can't see a sensible point.''

''Well, what *would* you do?''

''I suppose I'd come back the next day and take a hundred.''

''—and maybe steal Kate, too, if you were thirty years younger, eh, Lucius?'' Hawkins put in. Tight laughter rattled against the walls and Lucius Field waved a bony hand.

''I will admit I had never looked at the situation in exactly this light before, but . . .''

''How about it, Field?'' Fallon demanded. ''Will you go along with me?''

''I'll go along to the point of agreeing that some sort of action should be taken.''

''Asa Wheeler is with me,'' Fallon said.

When heads turned toward Wheeler for confirmation, he nodded. ''The sheriff's not just tooting a tin horn. We've got to do something. How do the rest of you boys feel?''

Fallon felt a surge of triumph as all of the other men, in one fashion or another, said that they would go along; the time had come to act.

''But have we any definite facts to go on?'' Field asked.

''My top hand's dead,'' Branneman said bitterly. ''That's a fact.''

''Now, Jed, don't get riled. I mean facts about the

identity of the night riders. They're—well, call them phantoms, spirits. The point is, they're faceless men. Who are they? Where do they come from?''

Wheeler spoke sarcastically. ''We all got a pretty good notion about that.''

''I'd be willing to lay money that Luke Mitchell and his crew are the night riders,'' Branneman said quickly.

''And that Mace Coldfield owns the Rocking L,'' came another voice.

''I've heard rumors to that effect myself,'' Field told them. ''I always look first for a source of trouble close to home. I will admit that the Mitchell spread is so rotten it smells to heaven. But I insist on one thing—is there proof?''

Fallon spoke in the heat of impatience and anger. ''What proof do we need? Let's go after Mitchell and his men. Arrest them. Force the truth out of them—''

''That's a rather quick move to make,'' Field said. ''After all, we could be wrong. What if the night riders are really men from somewhere outside the basin? Outlaws from up around Halstead? No, Sheriff, we may be resolved to fight, but we aren't resolved to start useless gunplay. Even if Mitchell's men weren't the night riders, there would certainly be gunplay if they were provoked.''

General sentiment, murmured among the others, was in agreement over this. Even Asa Wheeler went along with Field.

''Sheriff, I don't like to say this, but I've got to. You've got a personal stake in this fight. You can handle a gun better than most of us. But as I see it, you need our help. We need yours. Lord knows, you've opened our eyes, and

I don't give a curse about why you've done it. I see the sense in your ideas. But I do say you can't play a lone hand in this and start gunning down the Mitchell crew, even though we all believe that's where the trouble lies. Like Lucius, I don't want bloodshed if it's not necessary.''

Fallon drew a deep breath. He had almost known it would be this way, and though he did not like the idea, he resigned himself to it. ''All right, I'll go along on that.''

''What we need is proof that the night riders are Mitchell men,'' another rancher said.

''How do we get it?'' Oscar Hawkins queried, puzzled.

''The simplest way would seem to be to unmask one of the night riders,'' Lucius Field replied. His eyes went flinty again. ''If the face behind the sack belongs to a Mitchell man, then we use our guns. Not until then.''

''That'll take a bit of doing,'' Wheeler told them. ''The night riders are clever. Even though some of 'em have been wounded bad, the wounded are never left behind.''

''So we've got to catch one or more of them,'' Fallon said.

''Have you got some sort of idea worked out along those lines, Sheriff?'' Piney Woods wanted to know.

Fallon took a tight, deep breath. ''I have. We'll bait a trap for them.''

''Keep talking, Sheriff,'' Lucius Field said.

''As I understand it, most of you haven't moved many steers into Longhorn in the past months, have you?''

''We've been afraid to,'' Branneman told him. ''For spreads like the Box W here, it's easy enough—Asa's close to town. For the rest of us, out along the edges of the basin, it means a drive of two or three days. Which means

84

a couple of nights bedded down on the trail, with the cattle more skittish than usual. That's too good a chance for the night riders to hit us.''

''But a fairly large drive is just the bait we can use to draw out the night riders,'' Fallon went on to explain. He leaned forward intently. ''Here's the plan I figured out. Suppose a couple or three of you men from the edges of the basin decide to get up a herd for shipment. You let the word get around that you're not taking the cattle to Longhorn by the regular trail; you're moving them through Big Creek Cutoff. It's fourteen miles out of the way, but you figure if you move that way, secretly, you're safe from attack.''

''We wouldn't be, though,'' Oscar Hawkins said apprehensively. ''Big Creek Cutoff is an A-1 spot for the night riders to jump us.''

''Sure it is,'' Fallon agreed. ''The word that the cattle are moving through Big Creek—and when they are moving—would be secret, or supposed to be. Only there'd be a deliberate slip-up. We could find a hand from one of the spreads driving who's got a reputation as a loose talker when he's drunk—''

''I got a whole bunkhouse of them kind,'' a rancher said dryly. Others chuckled.

''Well, we'd send this hombre to the saloons to pass out information about the 'secret' drive when he's supposedly drunk. Send him to the Crystal. Let him spill his mouth all he wants. If Coldfield has a hand in the rustling, he'll get the word, and Mitchell and the riders will show at Big Creek on the night we pick.

''The cattle, though, won't be at Big Creek. We can

start the drive—or you can; I'll have to keep my name out of it, until the showdown—and then swing away from Big Creek and bed the herd down with a skeleton crew at a nearby ranch. Hawkins, your spread is near Big Creek, isn't it?''

''Right close, yes.''

''Good. Now we'll make it clear that the herd will bed down the first night at Big Creek, and when the night riders turn up, we'll be waiting. You can't refuse to use a gun on them if you know they're after your cattle. Our job won't be to kill as many as we can—'' Fallon's eyes flickered in the lamplight; the death's head expression sat on his face an instant—''but to capture one or two, dead or alive, and take the masks off them. If and when we find they're Mitchell's riders, the law can take a hand officially and we'll clean them out.''

Silence hung in the lamp-lit parlor for several seconds. The ranchers—not heroic men, but plain-faced, hard-knuckled workers who had fought a livelihood from the earth of the Washoe Basin—thought their own thoughts, or searched the faces of their neighbors for reaction. Branneman, running a restless hand through thinning hair, stood up.

''Forrester isn't going to die for nothing. I go along with the sheriff's plan. I'll have my cattle on that drive.''

''My spread's on the other side of the basin,'' another man said, ''but I've got a Winchester, and I'll be there at Big Creek.''

''Same goes for me,'' said a third voice.

The men surged to their feet, and Fallon's mouth split a harsh grin. He had done it. Lucius Field stepped forward.

"I venture you didn't think you would convince me so easily, Fallon."

"No! I didn't," Fallon agreed with him.

"You mistook logic for stubbornness. I'll ride with you at Big Creek." And he extended his raw-boned, leathery hand.

One by one they spoke, offering suggestions, until the plan took on more concrete form. The make-up of the herd was determined, the planted "drunk" selected, the date set. And through it all, Fallon's heart slugged furiously in his chest and he felt that before long, he would strike back at those who thought a professional lawman could be frightened into running.

CHAPTER XII

FALLON returned to Longhorn that night thoroughly satisfied. He was convinced that they had worked out a skillful
plan. Only those present at the meeting would know that
the coming drive to the cattle pens at the railhead was
being deliberately engineered to lure out the night riders.
None of the hands of the various ranches would be in on
the secret, except for Asa Wheeler's few trusted men who
were present when Fallon laid out the plan, plus one Hirsh
Martell, a wrinkled oldster who worked for Branneman.
In his role of the deliberately talkative drunk, Martell had
to be aware of the nature of the plan, but Branneman
insisted that the oldster could be trusted implicitly.

Otherwise, none of the hands who would be riding with
the herd would be aware of anything deeper than the fact
that the drive was supposed to be secret and go via Big
Creek Cutoff. At the last moment, a few of them would be
dispatched with the herd when it was turned off the trail
and driven to Oscar Hawkins' spread, while the rest of the

cowboys rode with the ranchers to wait in ambush. Keeping the cowboys in the dark as long as possible was a good way to avoid mishaps, Fallon and the others had felt.

" 'Sides," Asa Wheeler had spoken, "if one or two of 'em get likkered and spill what they know, that'll help our plan all the more. Provided—" Wheeler had stabbed the air with his finger for emphasis "—they don't know enough to really mess things up."

The date of the ambush had been set for the following Friday night.

As Tuesday and Wednesday passed in Longhorn, a peculiar quiet settled over the town. The weather became still and hot, with the sun scorching down from a windless, merciless blue sky. For the first time coming to Longhorn, Fallon had no drunks or rowdies in the tank on either Tuesday or Wednesday evening. As time passed the sheriff began to feel uneasy. What if something had gone wrong already? What if Hirsh Martell had gotten *too* drunk? Fallon, attempting to keep far away from the activities of the cattlemen, to safeguard the plan, made no inquiries about Martell. He did not know if the oldster had made his pre-arranged visit to the town's saloons yet. He had not seen Martell anywhere.

On Thursday afternoon, Fallon dropped in to the Boston. Tom Nash, playing a laconic game of stud in the hushed, drowsy air, pushed back his chair and came to join Fallon over a whisky at the bar.

"I'd swear Longhorn was becoming a ghost town," Nash told him as he poured a brace of shots from a bottle of his personal stock. Nash's eyes gleamed with quiet humor. "I sense something brewing, Sheriff."

"It has been quiet," Fallon agreed in a noncommittal tone.

"Actually, trouble in this town is none of my business, unless it occurs within the Boston here. But I would hate to lose a good sheriff. And I think perhaps you know why things are so quiet. Like the proverbial calm before the downpour."

"Storm," Fallon amended.

"It's hackneyed enough as it is," Nash said, grinning. He raised a second shot. "Cheers, as they do *not* say in Longhorn."

"I must get back to my game," Nash said as he finished his drink. "Whatever the forthcoming show is going to be, I think it should be entertaining to watch. But I have got some civic pride, strangely enough. So whatever your role, Mr. Fallon, play it carefully. The honest businessmen of Longhorn are grateful that things have quieted." And with a slight bow, Nash moved back to the green baize table and resumed his seat. Fallon lingered a moment longer at the bar, wishing that it were not Thursday but a day later. On the rear wall of the saloon, a large ornamental clock with an immense pendulum ticked monotonously, and out in the street could be heard the rising whine of a wind. . . .

On the way back to his office, Fallon met Chip Wheeler. The youth tried to push past him, but Fallon blocked his way.

"Something you wanted, Sheriff?" Chip asked insolently. His pale blue eyes were cold.

Fallon indicated the youth's gun belt. "I thought I'd better remind you not to play tough with that iron while you're in Longhorn. Stunts like you pulled out at the ranch won't make you very popular in these parts.''

"Thanks for the advice," Chip replied with contempt. His pale lips twisted. "But I don't give a hoot about being popular here. The sooner I shake the dust of this place from my boots, the happier I'll be." The youth stuck a cigarette in the corner of his mouth and lit a match with a flamboyant flourish. He looked sidewise, with hooded eyes, at Fallon. "And that may not be very long, either."

"Now what's *that* supposed to mean?" Fallon asked.

"You figure it out. Now, Sheriff, if the sermon's finished, I'm on my way to have a drink."

Fallon stepped out of the way and let Chip pass. Then, with a shrug, the sheriff turned and headed for his office. You could only do so much. . . .

CHAPTER XIII

THE wind rose on Thursday and whipped with keening violence through Longhorn, slamming doors, rattling windows, and blowing hats half a block or more. Dust settled on everything. Fallon, walking through the early darkness to his office, tasted the grit in his mouth and cursed. Why did even the elements seem to conspire to build up tension in a man? Gratefully, he opened his office door, but because he gripped the knob a bit loosely, it was blown from his grip and smacked back against the wall.

The shot-like noise caused Fallon to look up sharply. A figure stirred in the grayish light. Fallon stepped inside, peering, and closed the door. The wind whined and sang. Fallon's heart began to beat a little faster as Kate Wheeler stepped out of the shadows.

Closing the door, Fallon said awkwardly, "Why, hello, Kate. What brings you here?"

She indicated the grocery basket resting on his desk, but her smile was rather pale. The two of them were like phantoms in the tiny office, lost in a cloudy gray limbo while the wind howled and screeched outdoors. Her coppery hair had a blown look. He had never seen her look more beautiful. Particles of sand clung to his tongue and made it hard to speak.

"Did you know that Dad confided in me about your plan?" she asked.

"No, he didn't mention that," Fallon returned. "But there's no harm in your knowing, is there? I don't think you're the leader of the night riders." His banter fell flat.

Anxiously Kate Wheeler toyed with the ribbons of the hat she held in her hand. "Eli," she bit her lip, "I've called myself a dozen kinds of fool for coming here like this, but I had to."

"Why?"

"I don't approve of this drive." She hesitated breathily, shook her head. "That's not quite correct. Your idea about the night riders getting bolder if they're not opposed is sound and good. But I know why you are going into this. Your personal motive, I mean." Her eyes caught fire momentarily, and she flushed. "Here I am, blathering like a silly schoolgirl, and I've never done it before!

"Ever since the dance Saturday, I've pretended to myself that I didn't care what happened to you; that I hated the way you thought. But that's not true." She averted his eyes, faltering. "I'm too quick to speak, that's all."

Fallon smiled. "You spoke your mind the first night I came to Longhorn. You shouldn't change." Slowly, even a little hesitantly, he advanced toward her. The blood sang in his brain, boiled hot. The wind howled and drummed on the windows but no breath of air stirred in the darkening

93

office. "We're alike, Kate. We're honest and we do speak out. Now what's wrong with that?" Gently he took her shoulders in his hands.

She met his eyes squarely. "I care what happens to you. You might as well know it. I'm happy about it, and maybe a little ashamed, and mixed up and frightened . . . but a person is what he is."

"Why do you care?"

"What?"

"I wouldn't want you to care because you thought I was some sort of lost soul. I saw some mission singers in St. Louis once, with a street band. You're not like that, are you?"

She raised her face. "I . . ." Barely a whisper; her breath sweet against his face. "I'm not like that. I want you to be careful tomorrow night . . . for a different reason."

He caught her to him, kissed her, and she responded fiercely. Her mouth tasted fresh against his dusty lips. With his arms clasped tightly around her, he said, "If I can believe in you, I can believe that people aren't so bad after all, or so selfish. At least I think I can."

"I hope so," she whispered.

The kiss, when it was over, seemed such an utterly strange, delicate and wonderful thing that neither of them wanted to shatter its spell. Kate, still flushed, gathered up her basket and moved quickly toward the door. He held her hand for a moment, briefly, and then the wind blasted in through the opened door and she was gone, her face lingering before his eyes with its ripe, rich promise. He sat down at his desk and drew a deep breath.

"Whew!" he said softly, in awed wonder.

CHAPTER XIV

FRIDAY dawned gray, with the wind still tearing out of the sky. It did not soon let up, so that by nightfall, when Fallon rode quietly out of town via the back streets, he could hardly hear the hoofbeats of his own horse above the wind's furious scream.

He met the herd a mile short of Big Creek Cutoff. The wind amplified the muffled tramping of the hoofs, and carried to his ears the hoarse shouts of the cowboys, having a difficult time of it since the cattle spooked easily in the wild weather. The herd was being headed off east of a grove where the trail branched. Fallon galloped past the point, swung out along the fanning side of the rough triangle of flesh-on-the-hoof, by the swung riders and the drag men chewing the dust at the rear of the herd. A quarter of a mile behind the herd he met Asa Wheeler, Branneman, Somers, Teechford, Field and almost two dozen other ranchers and cowhands. Fallon reined in, noticing with grim approval that all the men were heavily armed.

"The herd's turned off for Hawkins' place," Wheeler shouted above the wind.

"Good," Fallon called back. "How many with them?"

"Skeleton crew. Less'n a dozen. Oscar's there. I sent Piney along, though he didn't want to go. Chip, too." Wheeler spat. "Danged nephew never was any good in a gunfight, for all his brass. How're things in town?"

"Quiet. Did Martell get the message across?"

"Spilled it in the Crystal last night," Teechford put in.

"Good. I didn't see him. I was worried. . . ."

Lucius Field, leaning tall in his saddle against the wind, a Winchester across his knees and his hat brim flapping, said, "All we need to worry about now are the night riders."

Fallon looked at the nearly dark sky. "We'd better ride, then."

The company moved off, going slowly to survey the terrain. Men lounged in the saddle, smoking cigarettes. Pairs of hawkish eyes scouted the hillsides for signs of watchers, but saw none. Fallon and Wheeler rode out ahead. The horses made little sound. Darkness had fallen almost completely when they reached Big Creek Cutoff; the trail here wound through a small circular basin surrounded by rather high hills. Fallon and Wheeler deployed the men to form a ring of guards around the edge of the little valley. In order to raid a herd supposedly bedded down by the trickling stream in the center of Big Creek Cutoff, the riders would have to come over the crests of the hills or in through the two slope-walled passes at either end of the small basin. Men were posted all around, bellied down in the grass, rifles by their sides, horses picketed in the brush ready for instant use. The ambush ring was spaced at good-sized intervals, so that a large band of horsemen could slip through between two ambushers without seeing either one. In other words, Fallon and Wheeler had organized a series of human fence posts around the Cutoff, but the fence was not strung. The night riders had to come into the trap.

Fallon and Wheeler took up posts on the opposite slopes of the south pass. Fallon chose that position because it lay closest to Mitchell's Rocking L. He hoped the night riders would come from that direction, to give further proof of his theory.

Darkness came. The wind began to decline to a low sob, then fell off to a whisper. Fallon's horse stirred in the brush behind him. A few insects rattled. Eight o'clock came. Then nine, ten, and eleven. Fallon lay cramped uncomfortably on the slope, his eyes growing accustomed to the darkness. Nothing stirred out by the creek. Nothing stirred all across the cup-like depression.

There was a rattling as someone came crawling through the brush at the foot of the slope. Fallon streaked for his colt, pulled it free, then relaxed as Asa Wheeler's voice called, "Don't get proddy, Sheriff. It's only me." The rancher came scrambling up the slope, puffing heavily. The two men hunkered down in the pale starlight that was beginning to show here and there through ragged openings in the cloud ceiling.

"What d'you think?" Wheeler asked uneasily.

A nagging worry pushed into Fallon's mind. As quickly, he pushed it away. "I think there's a lot more night ahead of us."

"It's blamed quiet." Fallon did not reply. Wheeler

cleared his throat and went on, "Starlight'll help us some."

"You're sure Martell put out the story in the Crystal?"

"Yes, Sheriff, Teechford told me himself. Some of Teechford's boys got it straight from a Three Cross hand who was there at the time. Martell made a big show of telling everybody that he knew the cattle would be moving through Big Creek Cutoff, and not by the regular trail like they usually did. There were even a couple of Mitchell men right in the place. Simms, the one who whinnies like a horse when he laughs, and another one. The Three Cross man saw 'em."

"Um." Fallon squatted in silence. The air had cooled with the darkness, and the smell of fresh earth and grass rose in his nostrils. He shivered unaccountably. He listened. The wind still talked a little, but beyond it lay only silence.

"I wish they'd show," Wheeler complained.

"They will," Fallon said, though worry was growing stronger now.

"Well, I better get back to my spot. Whistle if you sight something." And Wheeler crept off into the darkness.

Fallon wanted a cigarette in the worst way, but did not dare make a light. Another hour passed. The whole world lay dark and empty of sound; more stars peeped through, and Fallon thought he could make out the ghostly quicksilver trickle of Big Creek far below. Then he heard it.

Hoofbeats, their sound coming across the basin like soft drums.

"Fallon!" Wheeler's whispered catcall bounced from slope to slope.

"Yes."

"I hear it . . ." His spine crawled.

"Sound to you like what it sounds to me?" came Wheeler's raspy call.

"Yeah," Fallon called in reply. "Sounds like only one horse. *Let's ride.*"

He scrambled into the saddle as two shots ripped loudly through the night air. They came from down by the creek, followed after a pause by two more. Wheeler's mount clattered down the opposite slope alongside Fallon's, and the stocky rancher cried, "Sheriff, that's *our* warning signal, in case something goes wrong."

Fallon dug in his spurs and the two riders thundered toward the creek. In the darkness other men rode down from the hillsides. There was a noisy, milling group of riders on the other side of the creek. "Who is it?" Fallon shouted as they rode up. "What's wrong?"

Horses milled and whinnied. Men bumped against one another. Someone lit a match, and in the flaring orange glow Fallon saw the face of Piney Woods.

"Piney!" he exclaimed. "What the devil are you doing here?"

The small puncher, out of breath, gulped air into his lungs. "Sheriff," he gasped, "I had to ride here to get help."

"Speak up!" somebody yelled.

"The night riders!" Piney shouted. "Something went wrong! Not ten minutes ago, they attacked the herd at Hawkins' place!"

"Good Lord!" came one exclamation.

"And only a skeleton crew with them," Wheeler shouted.

Fallon wheeled his horse, sawing savagely on the reins.

He fought his way through the milling men, desperation driving him. The trap had closed—the wrong way. The other ranchers swung their horses and followed him. Hoofbeats shook the earth and wind whipped Fallon's face. They cut up the hillside and over, riding hell-for-leather, while Fallon hoped desperately they would not be too late. When they were less than a mile away from where the herd was bedded down, they began to hear the sound of gunfire.

CHAPTER XV

SWEEPING down over a low rise with Fallon in the lead, the ranchers spotted the scene of battle immediately. The thin, pale starlight showed a vast sea of heaving animal bodies and tossing horns, wraith-like between veils of dust. Through the confusion, men rode, firing at one another, the few cowhands bunched together in a tight little knot on the far side of the herd. About half of the night riders—a dozen or so men—shot it out from horseback with the cowhands, while the remaining raiders got the cattle moving away from the direction of the ranch. Shouts and curses interspersed with gunshots punctuated the night air. Bright spurts of gunflame etched tracks across the dark. The earth shook and vibrated as the cattle lurched ponderously into motion. In the whole wild, nightmarish scene, the most terrible sight was that of hooded forms on horseback, like demons out of hell.

Fallon lashed his horse at a furious pace. They were only men, he reminded himself, but the knowledge was bitter as gall. For he and the ranchers were on the defensive now, fighting to prevent this rustling raid from becoming chaotic defeat.

Clawing his Colt free, Fallon hunched in the saddle and swung his band of riders in a wide circle to the right, around the body of the herd. Riding in the opposite direction, to the left, would only have meant plunging directly into the path of the herd that was now on the move, even though slowly.

The defending cowhands saw help on its way and raised a hoarse shout. A group of the night riders whirled their horses and came at Fallon and his comrades full tilt. Having difficulty shooting from the saddle with much accuracy, Fallon nevertheless got off a pair of shots. Asa Wheeler also fired, as did the others. Lucius Field, his legs gripping his mount beneath him, rode tall as an Indian warrior, a stern figure of fury as he used both hands to fire his Winchester.

Through the dust and darkness Fallon thought he saw one of the night riders grab his belly and fall forward across his mount's neck, but he could not be sure. While the ranchers were still a good distance away, the night riders wheeled their horses again and went pounding off behind the cover of the moving herd. Fallon recognized the danger in the situation. The cattle, frightened by the gunfire and confusion, were being driven at a fast pace. Almost as Fallon thought this, Asa Wheeler gave the idea voice and called out:

"Goin' to be a stampede if somebody isn't careful . . . !"

The rest of his words blurred away under the thundering

boom of the trampling steers. Fallon and his group had reached the beleaguered cowhands, who had mounted up. Lucius Field cried out: "Look! They're forming a line of defense."

Fallon peered through the gloom, steadying his skittish horse. True enough. Nearly twenty of the hooded men had formed a solid wall of flesh and gun-iron midway across the pasture. The remaining rustlers yowled at the herd, urging it along past the line of defense. Words were not needed among the ranchers. They swung their horses into a gallop, firing from the saddle as they rode toward the defense line, which began to break up as a few of the night riders galloped forward also to get closer range.

The night exploded into a red-laced havoc. Bullets sang around Fallon as he rode, and his own Colt bucketed ferociously in his fist. Reloading from the saddle, he checked his horse momentarily to see what result the ranchers' charge had produced. Two night riders had been hit, but others of the marauding band had taken care that the wounded did not fall from their saddles. Four or five ranchers, including Teechford, were down too. Fallon saw Teechford lying in the dust, bloody holes drilled into his throat and out the back of his head. Wincing in hatred, Fallon heard Asa Wheeler shout:

"They're runnin' after the herd."

The battle, a series of stops and starts amid the near-darkness, now took up new motion. Since the herd was moving rapidly now, boiling up and away over rises from the pasture onto the prairie beyond, the defensive line had melted and the night riders were swinging off after the cattle, bent on escape. The ranchers plunged in chase.

Fallon rode with them for a moment, the wind singing in his ears, until he noticed that the ranchers had difficulty riding in a straight line of pursuit. They rode near the rear fringes of the herd, and had to be alert for sudden off-shoots from the herd that might block the path. One horse actually bolted into a knot of steers and its rider went down screaming over the tossing horns.

Having only one purpose now, to get his hands on one of the masked men and tear the disguise away, Fallon cut away from the main body of the ranchers and spurred his mount to the right. Here, relatively free from the danger of running into the cattle, he could ride faster. He swept out ahead of the ranchers and caught sight of a night rider who lagged a little behind his fellows. Fallon spurred for him. The night rider rode desperately, his hood flapping behind him. He turned in his saddle and pumped shots at Fallon. The bullets scorched narrowly by Fallon's face. Taking time to make his shot good, Fallon brought the night rider to the ground with three crashing shots that blasted a bloody tattoo across the man's chest.

Grimly triumphant, Fallon rode hard for the fallen man, but caught his breath sharply as he saw three other hooded riders double back toward him. Clearly they also were heading for the fallen rustler. Fallon threw himself out of his saddle and raced forward in a low crouch. Bullets sang and spat around him, chewing up the earth. Though he had not realized it before, he had worked his way back close to the fringe of the herd, and a solid stream of cattle rushed past not six feet to his left, deafening his ears with their hoofbeats.

He threw himself forward in a dive toward the dead

rustler just as the other three galloped up. One aimed a Winchester butt in a crashing blow at Fallon's skull, which the sheriff avoided only by a desperate, twisting roll to the side. He came up shooting. One of the hooded figures swayed in the saddle and cried out, but did not fall. Dazed, and slightly off balance, Fallon tottered for a moment and tried to wipe the grating dust from his eyes with the back of a sweated, grimy hand. With horror he saw a grim scene enacted before him.

Two of the night riders sawed back on the reins. Their horses pawed the air and came down hard. The grinding, tearing hoofs smashed the head of the man Fallon had dropped from his saddle. Rushing forward, Fallon found his gun empty again and paused to re-load. The third member of the band shot at him and he dropped behind a bush, feeling its scaly thorns tear his cheek. He rammed loads home with desperate swiftness, but already the night riders had gathered up the dead man, whose head and face had now been pounded to a bloody, featureless ruin.

''Throw 'im there,'' Fallon heard one of them call. *''Throw 'im!''*

Another leaped down, pulled the wounded man into the saddle, rode dangerously close to the edge of the herd and pushed the corpse free again. It dropped in the path of the cattle. The night rider fought his horse free again, as the third member of the group wheeled back to join his two companions.

''Damfool . . .'' came the third man's shout. But the damage had been done. Fallon caught a grisly glimpse of a ragdoll body being tossed on horns against the starlight. The other three night riders hesitated a moment too long also. The cattle swung out around them on both sides and hemmed them in. The three hooded men, a little island in the midst of the mad sea, tried to fight their way out of the herd that had engulfed them. Gunfire roared. Cattle screamed. The panicked steers began to run faster and stumbled into steers ahead of them. The three night riders crashed against one another as their horses reared. One by one they went down, clawing, their screams ringing in naked anguish above the thunder of hooves. The horses, gored and bleeding, pawed and lunged like mad things. Fallon lay behind the brush. Less than a foot away, cattle roared past, and he dared not move for fear of being trampled. But the cattle pushed harder now, and from a distance Fallon heard a voice he recognized as belonging to one of the ranchers. It floated in space for a moment, ripe with warning and hoarse terror:

"Stampede! *Stampeeeeede!*"

Like monsters, cattle appeared from the darkness and rushed past, bawling and howling like souls in torment. The ground shook until Fallon thought the world would fall apart. He buried his face in the dirt and kept his eyes open in slits, watching the fantastic rushing holocaust that swept past him. For endless hours it seemed to continue, and then at last the line thinned, until finally only a few straggling head lingered behind, and then none. Fallon rose to his feet and looked on up the basin where the animal juggernaut continued to roar forward. Noise retreated from him but remained an insistent thunder in the background.

Wearily, breathing deep, sweat pouring from every inch of his skin, he shoved his gun in his belt and walked forward, searching for the bodies of the night riders who had fallen.

Three had deliberately tried to wipe out beneath the slashing hooves the identity of a fourth who had fallen. Those three, bloody wrecks, had been killed with equal ferocity. Little that was human or even recognizable remained of the four raiders. A wad of red flesh; a scrap of feed sack with blood around the eyehole. . . .

Fallon was retchingly sick in the brush.

A moment later, he felt better. Again he wiped the salty sting from his eyes. Not too far away, he spotted his horse and limped wearily toward it. Mounting up, he rode in the direction the stampede had taken. In several minutes he met a cowhand he recognized as working for Branneman.

"What's happened?" Fallon asked tersely. "Where are the rest of the ranchers?"

The cowhand snickered, but without humor. "Chasing the steers. I was sent back to Hawkins' place to get a buckboard for them that are hurt."

"Stampede look like it would run itself out?"

"Eventual. Forked off into three forks. Them night riders herded off the steers in the middle; our men took the rest. You might ride on up. Over that rise. I imagine they could use some help."

So *could I*, Fallon thought bitterly.

"Obliged," he said, and rode off.

He got his breath back, and across the rise ran into three more riders who were chasing strays. "Wheeler's trying to mill 'em up ahead," one of the hands informed Fallon, who rode on. Before long, he joined Wheeler and the other ranchers who had succeeded in getting some of the cattle started running in a circle that wound inward. Once the ranchers succeeded in doing this, the force of the stampede wore itself out. Fallon helped the hands gather the steers in an orderly herd, and they drove the cattle back toward the Hawkins spread. Fallon worked and rode mechanically, for he was aware of the bitter sting of defeat.

CHAPTER XVI

NEAR dawn, the dirty, bedraggled survivors gathered in the kitchen of the Hawkins ranch house and drank from a pot of coffee Mrs. Hawkins had brewed. Through the windows, as the eastern sky lighted, Fallon could see the cattle bedded down peacefully once more. It was as though the whole thing had not happened. Yet it had. Every terrible moment was etched on Fallon's brain, like a picture on the plate of one of those new-fangled photo gadgets.

Fallon washed his cup in a pail of water and set the cup on the table. The lamps flickered as a slight wind blew through the open kitchen door. No one had said much. All were too tired, too defeated. Reluctantly, Asa Wheeler raised his eyes from his own cup of coffee.

''How many *did* they get?'' Fallon asked.

''Eight, nine hundred head, near as we can calculate,'' Wheeler said. Fallon had wanted to organize a group of men to chase the rustled herd. He gave up that idea once he saw the faces of the ranchers. There were weary, beaten for the moment. Not a man of them, he suspected, would have stirred now, after the crushing defeat. It would not have been so bad if they had not expected to be successful in capturing the night riders. But they had not anticipated an utter rout.

"How many of our men are dead, Asa?" Lucius Field asked somberly.

"Five. Chancey Vought may not live either. About a half dozen more wounded."

"And nobody got a look at the face of one of the night riders? Not a one of you?" Fallon demanded.

Silence.

The wind whispered through the doorway. The lamps burned lower. In the east the sky turned milky.

"They killed their wounded," Lucius Field said.

"Or carried 'em off," spoke up Somers. "It looks like you can't hardly beat them."

Suddenly, from beyond the closed kitchen door, came the agonized sound of a woman's muffled sobbing.

The kitchen door opened. Mrs. Hawkins came in and caught her husband's eye. "Oscar," she said softly, "it's Emmy Teechford. She's come for her husband's body. Would a couple of you men . . ."

Hawkins, a smear of dirt on his bald forehead, nodded and walked out of the room. Two others followed. The door closed. Lucius Field stood up and said to no one in particular, "I think I'll ride home." He went out through the back door, and in twos and threes the remaining ranchers followed.

Wheeler said solicitously, "Ride on back to town, Sheriff. You look like you could use some rest."

"I could use a lot more than that," Fallon said bleakly, thinking how close he had been to capturing one of the rustlers. But he said goodbye, mounted up and rode back to Longhorn through the fresh, moist dawn. He tumbled into bed at Mrs. Clay's and slept till noon. Then he went around to the office to find Kate Wheeler waiting for him.

She rose to meet him with concern in her gray eyes. "Eli . . ."

He looked away miserably. "Did your dad tell you?"

She nodded. "Don't take it so hard! With six men dead . . ."

She shook her head.

"What?" He was startled.

"Chancey Vought . . . he worked for Branneman . . ."

"He died?"

"About nine this morning."

Fallon slammed a fisted hand on the desk.

Less than a week after the battle, seven strangers arrived in the Basin. Three of them, seen by a rancher who related the story to Fallon, rode in from the southwest, whip-lean men with leathery skin and bleak eyes, who wore gaudy ornamental spurs of Spanish silver and boasted a pair of guns apiece—even though each one, in the manner of most professionals, probably only used one at a time. They rode leisurely into the valley, shoulders bowed in contemptuous repose, and they glowered cynically at the rancher when they passed him. Before long, Fallon saw them in Longhorn.

He had traveled among that breed of men long enough to recognize his own half-brothers who wore no badges. The three gunslingers went to work for Luke Mitchell's

Rocking L. Four more, arriving in pairs on successive evenings on the six-thirty via the capital, also drifted out to the Mitchell spread. All four, dudishly dressed, sported derbys of the sort Fallon had worn. They, too, appeared at the bar in the Crystal one evening, as members of the Rocking L crew, in denims and range hats, their guns packed low and their hard eyes polished by redeye to a killing luster.

Fallon was not blind to the meaning of this. To him, it was a tacit admission on Mitchell's part that the Rocking L had met opposition at Big Creek; Mitchell ran the night riders. Fallon felt this more strongly than ever now. Why else, a week after the battle, did imported gunhands— who, Fallon knew, would come only at a high price —turn up? The seven men were seen on the ranges, indifferently going about the duties of cowhands. But any man might pick up that knowledge in six months' time. Mitchell wasn't paying them to ride herd on the slim stock he kept on the Rocking L lands.

"Seven gunnies," Asa Wheeler said to Fallon one night in town, shaking his head sadly. "I dunno, Sheriff. Makes a feller pause for a minute. You know Mitchell wouldn't hire amatoors—he knows what kind of an hombre you are, for one thing." At this, Fallon smiled the death's head smile. "The next fight, if there is one," Wheeler hastily amended, "is going to be a lot more dangerous."

"How do the ranchers feel?" Fallon asked.

"Pretty glum," Wheeler admitted. "The starch's gone out of most of 'em. We're right back where we were before you planned that ambush, only more so. Lucius

Field has thought it over, and he's against any more action—there may be more slip-ups, he says. He's got a point.''

Fallon cursed. ''Yes, but . . .''

''I know, I know!'' Wheeler waved. ''You don't have to sell *me* that bill o' goods all over again. I'm convinced the situation needs action more than ever. But I'm only one man, representin' one spread. With Lucius Field sitting tighter'n ever, it's going to be hard to get the rest of the men organized again. Besides, Emmy Teechford's half out of her mind with grief. Raves and screams around her place all day.'' Wheeler averted his eyes. ''You can't blame her, even if she is wrong in what she says. Well, never mind.''

''What does she say?'' Fallon demanded calmly.

''Like I told you,'' Wheeler hedged, ''she's wrong, and she'll realize it sooner or later. But a hysterical woman can make a man do a heap of thinking.''

''You still haven't told me what she's saying,'' Fallon replied.

Wheeler swung up on his horse and gazed out at the sunny sky with vacant nervousness. ''One of my boys told me she stays locked up in her house, but he heard her screamin' when he rode by, calling you a murderer.''

Flustered and unhappy that Fallon had pried loose the truth, Wheeler spun his horse around and sped up the street out of town.

CHAPTER XVII

LATE one evening Fallon stopped in the Crystal for a drink. Mace Coldfield came down from his office and made it a point to stop to converse. Fallon refused the saloon owner's offer of a drink. Coldfield shrugged, his greenish eyes shrewd and speculative, making a dangerous combination when coupled with the determination in his square, stocky face.

"I wouldn't want to compromise your honor as a peace officer by having you accept a drink on the house," Coldfield said with false affability. "Not if you don't want it that way."

"Have you something on your mind, Coldfield?"

"Do I usually?"

"From the times we've met, I'd say yes."

Coldfield extracted a cigar from his flowered vest, inserted it in his mouth and executed another shrug. "I'm merely curious. I have yet to receive a first-hand account of the fight out at Hawkins' place. The night riders, wasn't it?"

"Yes," Fallon said.

"Did you meet with much success, Sheriff?"

"Not as much as we'll have next time."

"Um." Coldfield sipped an ambery shot. "You say 'we'? You're cooperating with the ranchers, then?"

"I don't think I have to pass that information along to you."

"I don't quite understand. I haven't heard it before."

"Maybe not. I don't particularly care, either." Fallon finished the drink he had purchased with his own money and prepared to leave.

"I wish you luck in your campaign against the night riders," Coldfield said, raising his shot glass. Every glint in his sea-green eyes, every intonation of his voice gave the lie to his words. His rather heavy voice seeped and oozed with mockery and clever double meaning. Fallon left the saloon without even a curt word of farewell. After he had faced Mitchell, he would still have Coldfield to deal with. As if his stomach had a memory of its own, it convulsed and tightened, exactly as if Fallon were waiting to go for his gun in another instant. The noises of the main street dwindled as he moved along under the trees toward Mrs. Clay's. He kept going over the words of Mitchell and Coldfield in his mind. They had said, "We're innocent." They had meant, "You haven't got much longer till your string runs out."

Next day, following the lull after the raid, the first link in a long chain of events was forged; a link which was to lead Fallon to his last most desperate battle with three foes: with Luke Mitchell, with Coldfield, and with himself.

Old Man Pothwaite, who had a tiny farm east of Longhorn, was a sort of crank character in the basin. When he reported that his one horse, a sway-backed farm plug named Prairie Belle, had been "rustled," Fallon investigated the report. He did not want to humor Pothwaite so much as he wanted a short relief from the nerve-wearing job of trying to plan ahead against Mitchell and Coldfield. So Fallon rode out to Pothwaite's place, and found that Prairie Belle had been "rustled" to a creek half a mile from Pothwaite's back yard. Evidently it was the work of some prankish youngsters in town, for Prairie Belle was tied placidly to a tree by the creek, and a message had been carved laboriously on the tree trunk with a pen knife: "Yah! Go to blazes, Old Man Pothwaite!" The oldster took his horse and departed for his farm. Fallon turned his horse's head along the creek bank, enjoying the peaceful coolness of the trees. Sunlight drew a tracery on tinkling water, and the morning had the refreshing smell of green earth about it.

Rounding a bend in the creek, Fallon thought he saw someone on a horse, screened by the trees several hundred yards up on the bank. He could not clearly distinguish the figure, but it seemed to be rather slight. His horse moved through the crackling brush as he warily made ready to slap leather, if necessary. A bird twittered in the branches overhead. The horse behind the brush screen stamped and blew skittishly.

"Hello!" Fallon called cautiously, somehow sensing that this was not danger of the physical, lead-slug sort he was used to.

The horse in the brush reared, whinnied and bolted.

The animal crashed through the brush screen and raced toward Fallon along the bank. Fallon saw a flash of ebony hair, wind-tossed and gleaming in the sunlight. A white face blurred toward him in the dappled green-and-gold undergrowth. The horse was racing toward him at a fast clip, spooked, and Fallon switched his attention instantly from horse and rider to an obstacle directly in the path of the runaway. A limb hung down from a thick-boled tree that grew along the creek slope, and if the runaway horse kept galloping directly forward, the limb would strike the unsuspecting rider at throat level.

Fallon's awareness of the situation flicked into being in a tenth of the time it takes to tell. He uttered a hoarse, "Look out! Look out for that limb!" At the same moment he sicked his own mount forward in a burst of power. Fallon ducked his head, shot under the limb, hooked an arm around the waist of the other rider and dragged her from the saddle scant moments before her head might have been smashed to a pulp on the thick limb.

Fallon pulled his horse up, struggling to keep his balance. The woman—for the first blurred picture had been confirmed—seemed limp in his arms. Only by supporting her tightly beneath the arms across the back did he prevent her from falling. Her eyelids were closed and she appeared to be breathing with an effort. Lowering her until her heels touched the ground, Fallon found himself bent half out of his saddle in a cramped, awkward position which was hellishly uncomfortable. In the distance, the runaway mount slowed, the crashing noises died and the sounds of birds pushed through the stillness once more.

"You're all right!" Fallon said sharply, commandingly. He was irritated.

India Coldfield opened her eyes.

As she swayed on her feet and clung tightly to Fallon's arm, sunlight touched her ivory cheeks, and highlighted the blue shadows beneath her eyes. Her wine-colored velveteen riding gown, lacily frilled and altogether out of place here, showed dirt stains and large ugly rents in several places.

Fallon released his grip and straightened up in the saddle. India Coldfield, not speaking, assumed a hurt pout. She took a step toward a fallen log, and one foot seemed to twist awkwardly beneath her. She uttered a soft, "Oh!" and caught herself against the log as she fell, taking care, though, to arrange her skirts once she was seated. For a long moment she looked up at the sheriff who perched high above her in the saddle. Fallon was beginning to understand.

"Well," India Coldfield demanded, faintly petulant. "Aren't you going to help me? I think my ankle might be sprained."

Fallon eased himself down from the saddle. India Coldfield's red lips parted in a smile. As he walked toward her, Fallon had the feeling that the woman resting on the log could be as dangerous in her own way as any gun-slinger in Mitchell's crew.

He knelt, and she pulled her skirts up a bit so that he could make his examination.

"It's my ankle," she repeated. "It hurts terribly." Her voice bubbled with a triumph she could not conceal.

CHAPTER XVIII

KNEELING before India Coldfield in the dappled-green cool of the glade, Fallon touched his fingers to her ankle. Her flesh was warm above the shoetop, but he could detect no swelling anywhere. He raised his eyes in a sharp, quizzical expression, and saw her head framed by a whispering canopy of trees.

"Can you tell?" she inquired laughingly. "Is it really sprained?"

"Just a second more," he replied grimly.

He fastened his hands on both sides of her ankle, hesitated as if still feeling for a swollen place, and then wrenched sharply, twisting her ankle not enough to injure it, but enough to make her feel it. Ducking backwards, he scrambled to his feet. India Coldfield likewise leaped up, her black eyes shot with thunderbolts of rage. In an instant she realized she had made a wrong move, for she looked down quickly and her cheeks went scarlet. She was standing solidly on both feet, tiny white fists clutched angrily against her sides.

Fallon let loose a flat laugh.

India Coldfield took a few angry steps toward the tingling creek and whirled around. "It wouldn't take much to make me dislike you."

"Maybe not. But I'm wondering why you change your tune so quickly."

For a second it looked as though she would rush away through the trees, to find her horse and ride off in a furious gallop. Fallon took his time as he took a cigar from his vest, scrawled a match across a tree trunk and drew smoke. He flipped the match away. India Coldfield's shoulders trembled visibly beneath the wine-colored fabric of her dress. If a struggle was going on within her between angry admission of defeat and coquettish denial, denial won. For her eyebrows arched delicately and she assumed a gay manner once more.

She returned to the fallen log and sat down. "Can't we forget it? I'll admit my ankle might not have hurt as much as I said, but you never can tell about injuries like that, now can you? I'm not used to such a rugged existence."

Fallon's smile thinned. "Do you often go riding so far from Longhorn?"

She sighed. "What else is there for me to do in that hole? I go positively insane in that house all day."

"I don't think your horse spooked by accident."

"Look here. . . ." Again her eyes flamed; again she confronted him with clenched fists.

"I'm not saying for sure," Fallon amended, trying to fathom the reason for her being out here; the *real* reason. "I'm only saying that it looks awfully peculiar when I happen to be in the right place to give you a hand. It could happen by chance, but did it?"

"You've caught me again," she said. The harsh lines of her face relaxed somewhat. "I was out riding, I caught sight of you from a distance as you came down to the creek with that dirty old man . . ."

"Pothwaite."

"Yes. I rode along the creek to meet you. There was something in the brush that frightened my horse . . . a snake perhaps, I don't know." She shuddered a bit, then raised her eyes in quiet defiance. "Are you going to call me a liar on that score too?"

Fallon shifted uncomfortably. He understood a little more now. "I reckon it's not important."

"I wanted to talk to you, Mr. Fallon." She moved a step closer, moistening her lips. Her voice dropped throatily. "Perhaps I arranged that accident, perhaps not. Does it matter?"

Fallon shrugged. "What did you want to talk to me about?"

"Does that matter either?"

She sighed softly and rested her cheek against his shoulder. "Now what are you thinking, Sheriff?"

"That you're still Mrs. Mace Coldfield."

She laughed. "Then I see I'll have to be more persuasive. Very well. Perhaps I'd better look for my horse. But I warn you, Mr. Fallon, I won't give up easily. Whether you like it or not, you're fair game." She caught up her skirts and started off down the creek bank, her head held high as if she had won a sweeping victory.

CHAPTER XIX

Two nights later, he was sitting idly in his office and wondering whether it was worth getting wet to cross the street for a drink. The office had a dank, chilly smell about it. Rain hammered on the roof and turned the main street outside to a seething river of gluey brown mud. The windows creaked and whined. The rain had been falling since noon and Longhorn was quiet, the saloons nearly empty.

He pulled his hat down tight against the storm and left the office. Thunder cracked and rolled. Pools of standing water in the street turned to sheeted silver in the lightning's flicker. Inside the Boston saloon, life moved slowly. One bartender dozed. Three men and a house dealer were engaged in a lazy game of faro. One old-timer, bowlegged and bleary-eyed, crooned a wordless song to himself while leaning over the bar. In the comparative comfort of a lighted place away from the storm, the old man dreamed of nights like this on the long, lonely range. All the while he stared into a schooner of beer. Against the rain could be heard the whisper-flick of the faro dealer turning cards out of the box.

"Nash around?" Fallon asked the bartender.

"In the office." The bartender was too sleepy even to jerk a thumb.

Fallon touched his hat, walked to the rear of the saloon and knocked on a closed door. "Enter!" came Nash's mildly sardonic voice.

Fallon walked into the office. Nash, an expression of pleasant surprise on his long face, stood up behind his desk. "Fallon! I didn't expect to see you out in this weather. Longhorn is positively tomblike tonight. Have a chair and I'll break out my private stock."

Fallon murmured his thanks. He did not mind accepting a drink from this man. Nash laid the book he had been reading on the desk and set out a decanter and tumblers. Fallon idly noticed the book's title. *Walden*, it was called, by a man named Thoreau. Fallon had never heard of it.

Nash raised a tumbler, the amber liquid shot with glowing lamplight. "Ah!" He sighed deeply. "Liquor is the perfect companion for a dull, wet evening. Let's drink ourselves into a pleasant haze, shall we?"

Fallon had a tight smile on his face. "I'm afraid this isn't exactly a social call, Nash."

"No?" Nash shrugged pleasantly. "I should have known by that determined look on your face. What is it this evening? A catalogue of the sins of Luke Mitchell? Some personal advice? As an educated man from Harvard

University, I am completely unqualified to speak on any subject except saloonkeeping.'' Nash grinned. "Cheers.'' He drank.

"Do you know much about Chip Wheeler?'' said Fallon slowly.

Nash frowned, balancing the tumbler between his palms. "Chip Wheeler. Asa Wheeler's nephew? I don't know him personally, but I know who he is.''

"Does he come in here often?''

Nash touched his chin thoughtfully. "Now I don't know if you could say 'often.' He comes in perhaps once or twice a week. It's his custom, I believe, to visit every saloon in town at least once each week. Evidently he feels he ought to help the poor saloonkeepers of Longhorn not only meet their overhead, but to make a slight profit besides. He drinks heavily, or he always does when he's in here. From the few times I've noticed him, I'd say the liquor makes him a bit green around the gills. I think he's suffering from a common youthful failing. He imagines that hard drinking and the wearing of a gun necessarily make him better than other men.'' Nash's voice lost a little of its smooth, rich humor. "He strikes me as already being on the way toward developing into a loud-mouthed bully.'' The smile fleeted back. "Forgive me for rattling. But Chip Wheeler is always conspicuous.''

"Does he hang out mostly at the Crystal?''

"He goes there oftener than other places, yes.''

Fallon paused, framing his next question. "When you've seen him, has he ever displayed much money?''

Waving his tumbler, Nash frowned a bit. "Now there's a peculiar thing. I was about to remark on it. How old is that boy? Nineteen, perhaps twenty? And yet he flashes a bankroll that most men wouldn't have after a year's work on the range. Does Wheeler pay high wages?"

"No higher than most," Fallon replied. Yes, it was coming clear: a pattern that plunged him still deeper into worry and dismay.

"I've gathered that Asa Wheeler doesn't think much of the boy either," Nash commented.

"No, he doesn't," Fallon said, half-aloud. He perked up. "Does Chip always have a lot of money?"

"Always? I don't know how much he displays when he's in the Crystal or the Winding Trail. But in the Boston—" An emphatic nod. "Always. The men who come in here don't appreciate having money waved under their noses. When the boy gets a drink or two in him, he gets obnoxious. Another thing . . ."

"Yes?"

"One of his favorite topics of conversation is how he hates Longhorn and everything connected with the cattle business."

"Um." Fallon lapsed into silence for a moment.

"Sheriff . . ."

"What?"

"You're interested in Chip Wheeler."

"Well . . ."

"I'm curious as to why."

Fallon waved. "It's nothing. I was just checking on the way he acts. For his uncle."

Nash smiled. Without malice, he said, "Sheriff, a man needs higher education to become a skillful liar. Believe me, a classroom in which the difference between a passing mark and failure is determined by how tactfully the student agrees with the professor's point of view teaches a lesson that can profitably be applied to skulduggery. In plain lingo, you're giving me a line."

Fallon's eyes were somber sockets in his head. "All right, I am. I think Chip Wheeler may have some connection with the night riders."

Nash whistled low. "I see. Yes! I've always thought that the boy's income could hardly come from honest sources, but beyond that, I never dreamed!"

Fallon stood up abruptly. "Nash, I'm only telling you because I know I can trust you, and because you've helped me. Maybe I'm wrong. I hope that I am. I can't say anything else until I've done more nosing around. Fair enough?"

Nash chuckled. "Eminently. I'm still in your debt for the way you quieted this town. I haven't had a piece of furniture broken since you arrived on that six-thirty train."

"I'll be moving along, then."

"All right. Keep in touch. I get bored checking ledgers and liquor supplies all day long. I like to see excitement . . . no." Nash grew serious. "There, I'm doing the lying. Killing isn't good. Sometimes it's the only means to a given end, and is inevitable. But that still doesn't make it good." Across the polished, gleaming expanse of desk, Nash concluded, "And the way it looks to me now, there's going to be more killing."

"On that," Fallon told him, "you can bet your last dollar." And Fallon, too, had no idea of humor in his mind.

Nash picked up the book by Thoreau, and Fallon left. He had another drink at the bar. He had thought that Chip Wheeler might sell out if the price were high enough. But now Fallon had more than a theory: he had a witness who could state that Chip usually carried more money than he was normally entitled to have. There would surely be other witnesses. Grimly satisfied, Fallon went out into the street. The rain had slackened off to a thin drizzle. Once back in his office, he sat down in his chair, facing the front door as usual, propped his boots on the desk top and lit a cigar. In spite of having more than theory to go on, he had to plan his next move carefully. . . .

A number of things contributed to what happened next: the lulling splash of rain overhead, lending a false sense of security; the chill creeping slowly into the office, while the last chips and blocks guttered to red ash within the iron stove; the weight of worry that rested on Fallon's mind as he tried to determine how to prove a theory as truth. Time continued to tick away. Ten-thirty. Ten-forty. Then the hour, and soon a quarter past. A cigar smoldered on the edge of the desk, teetered and fell. Fallon half-dozed, eyes shut, fighting off sleep.

His nerves clanged an alarm a second too late.

There was already a gun barrel jammed cold and hard against the back of his neck.

Automatically, Fallon came awake and stiffened, even as his brain stopped further action when he felt the cold bite of the gunmetal against his skin. Simultaneous with his stirring in the chair, a voice made a soft, sharp syllable of warning, an utterance that told him the gun at his neck meant business: "Ah!"

Fallon put his hands on his knees and tried to turn his head just a bit.

"No sudden moves, please, Sheriff," said the voice. "I wouldn't want to splatter your brains out through your mouth."

Fallon's gray-blue eyes grew steely. "What the devil is this, Coldfield?"

"Sorry," Mace Coldfield replied in a chilly tone. "I'm doing this my way. Now stay seated and I'll come around in front of you so we can talk. I know you're fast, but I can pull this trigger in half the time it takes you to reach."

"I'm not loco enough to try it," Fallon told him.

"Not loco enough for that, maybe," Coldfield echoed. He circled Fallon and glared down, anger burning high in his greenish eyes. Bareheaded, his blond hair was wet, and his square, stock face had a beefy red hue. "But loco. You made a fool's mistake tonight, Sheriff."

"Since when have you taken to sneaking through the alley?"

"Since there's a professional gunman wearing a badge. I like the odds in my favor."

"Is this a business visit?" Fallon wanted to know. His stomach was coiled into a tight knot.

Coldfield's reddish face grew darker still. He waved the gigantic Colt clutched in one rock-knuckled fist. "Shut your mouth! I said I'd run this show."

Fallon lifted his hands a half inch off his trousers and shrugged. That motion caused Coldfield to draw back the Colt hammer. Alert green lights glinted in Coldfield's eyes. Fallon could easily see that Mace Coldfield had quick responses. Coupled with his ace-high hand in this situation, it meant trouble.

"If you want to put that iron away," Fallon said, still speaking flatly, and testing his opponent, "maybe we can thrash things out. I warn you, Coldfield, I don't like this."

Coldfield's lips peeled away from his teeth and he brayed harshly. "Isn't that too bad! For once you're on the receiving end. Sheriff, I've wasted enough time. Why are you nosing in my affairs?"

Fallon leaned forward, his eyes smashing against Coldfield's wrathful gaze. "Let's not play games. You're afraid I'm getting too close to the truth."

"Truth?" Coldfield frowned warily.

"Now you're trying to play dumb. You're behind the night riders. You own the Rocking L and you own Luke Mitchell. You're afraid I might be getting to know too much about your affairs. You're afraid your wife might have said something, told me straight out that you did own the Rocking L."

"No." Coldfield shook his head doggedly, but the reply was not convincing. "That isn't it. . . ."

"I think otherwise." Fallon rushed on, the words spilling hotly forth, one after another. "What's the reason, Coldfield? Does your wife bleed you? Is she too expensive? Is she too fancy? Is that why you hired yourself a crew of outlaws?"

For one brief instant, admission flitted across Mace Coldfield's face.

Coldfield recovered swiftly, cleared his throat and hefted the Colt. His voice smoothed out. "If I were behind the night rider raids, Fallon—you still wouldn't have a chance. You're fighting a one man war. The ranchers are yellow. Like ninety-nine percent of the human race, they're weak, every last man Jack of them. If I did own

Mitchell, you still couldn't beat the combination.''

The rain splattered on the windows, more lightly now.

"Have you answered my first question, Fallon?''

"I don't aim to.''

"Keep away from my property! Stay away from India! The next time I hear of you on my place, I'll shoot you down and I'll have every man in Longhorn on my side. But I don't suppose a man like you has ever heard of the unwritten law.''

"Why,'' Fallon said in the softest of voices, "I didn't expect that.''

"What?''

"A warning. I thought you were going to kill me right now.''

Coldfield stiffened. Fallon watched the saloon owner's trigger finger. The flesh along the stocky man's jaw quivered. "Damn you . . .'' he breathed.

"No. I wouldn't. You couldn't make it across the street. If you want to kill me, you'll have to send more of your hired gunnies to do it.''

Coldfield scowled, seemed to hesitate, and at last saw the truth of what Fallon said.

With a deep breath, he holstered the gun. Then he loosened the buckle below his waist and clanked the gun belt down on the desk.

"I can't kill you with a gun,'' he said heavily. "But I can use my hands to give you a lesson.''

Fallon stood up, feeling the cold touch of fear that came before every battle. With his heart racing in his chest, he unfastened his own gunbelt and hung it over the back of the chair. Coldfield tore away his string tie, shucked out of his coat and hat and pushed back his sleeves.

Ghoulishly, Coldfield grinned.

"Where do you want to fall, Sheriff? In the alley?"

"That will suit me fine."

Coldfield led the way, his boots thudding hollowly on the plank floor. They passed the cell row and went out through the open rear door. Fallon stepped down into thick mud. Off in the darkness, his horse stamped and blew. A thin, chilling mist of rain touched Fallon's cheeks. Idly he wiped the back of his hand across his mouth. He breathed faster. The only light here fell through the back door, a dim, watery reflection from the front of the office.

Mace Coldfield walked three paces down the alley, turned and chuckled, a thoroughly cold sound of grim pleasure. In the darkness, Fallon heard him call softly, mockingly, "Ready?" Fallon figured the odds. Coldfield out-weighed him by at least thirty pounds. The outcome of this was far from certain, and Fallon knew it.

He called back, "Any time you are."

CHAPTER XX

As THOUGH he had perfect confidence in his ability to beat
Fallon, Mace Coldfield moved forward warily, in a sort of
sidestepping shuffle, his arms hanging tense at his sides
and a half-smile shadowy upon his lips. Fallon circled to
his right and Coldfield repeated the movement, complet-
ing the circle. They began like a pair of bowie fighters,
lacking only the knives. Fallon tested his footing as he
shifted. The mud sucked and gurgled beneath his boots.
Tricky. . . .

Abruptly Coldfield lunged, swinging a roundhouse
right. Fallon dodged back, but not far enough. Coldfield's
fist slammed painfully along Fallon's right cheek. Coldfield bore in, arms widespread, but Fallon eluded the
trap. He jabbed a vicious left at Coldfield's face, and the
saloon owner reeled a step away, grunting. It was an
animal sound mingled with the pulpy noise of the blow
landing. Blood trickled from Coldfield's nose. Fallon
pounded a right to Coldfield's head, then another left. The

saloon owner absorbed the blows on the cheek and neck, letting his massive strength protect him. Before Fallon could leap away, Coldfield snorted and brought his knee flashing up. Jerking backward, Fallon was struck not in the groin but in the belly. He gasped momentarily, weakened. Coldfield rushed at him, poised for another grappling bear hug, but Fallon managed to drag himself out of the way, spin, bring up his own foot and send Coldfield down into the mud with a curse.

The massive man rose to one knee and daubed at the slime on his forehead. Fallon breathed rapidly. The strategy was becoming hellishly clear. Coldfield did not depend on quick, effective punches. He would try for a body hold, where he could use his power to crush. Fallon could not counteract or match thirty additional pounds of brute strength. He had to punch, and move fast. Too, Coldfield did not know the meaning of a clean fight, but that Fallon had anticipated.

Slowly Coldfield picked himself up. Fallon waited, recovering from the blinding hurt of the belly kick. Before he rose to full height, Coldfield threw himself forward in a flying dive. He managed to catch Fallon's left leg and hang doggedly on. Fallon rocketed down a blow against Coldfield's face, but it did not faze the man. With a hand on Fallon's belt, Coldfield twisted quickly and threw his shoulders against Fallon's legs. Fallon tumbled and struck the mud. Coldfield came heaving up over him, thick fingers reaching for Fallon's neck. Fallon struck the hands aside. Coldfield struck again, his knuckles pounding the side of Fallon's head. Down in the mud, Fallon tasted the gummy dirt. Coldfield leaped to his feet, and while he raised a foot to stamp down, Fallon summoned all his strength, braced his hands under him and also came swiftly erect.

"If I get my hands on you . . ." Coldfield rasped. "Just once . . ."

Fallon triphammered three blows to Coldfield's unprotected belly. The man had no fighting guard, but the stomach punches, though they made Coldfield wheeze and blink a little, seemed to have little serious effect. Coldfield's boot caught Fallon's shin in a savage kick. Like some mechanical man, Coldfield raised his hands again, grimly pressing for a stranglehold. Fallon unloosed a right that spun Coldfield half around. Two more punches sent Coldfield staggering against the plank wall of the office.

Conscious of a numb ringing in his head, and a salty taste of blood welling from a cut in his mouth, Fallon punched hard at the figure of the big man targeted against the wall. Coldfield, stunned by the blows, took them for a moment, and then gave his head a shake, like a wounded animal coming to its senses and gathering rage. Coldfield ducked a blow, and with speed surprising in so large a man, scooped up something from the mud. His arm swung in a wide arc.

Fallon found out that Coldfield had taken up a large, jagged rock. It connected with his head. The alley tilted crazily.

Coldfield seized Fallon's head between his thick hands and wrenched. This time, too, his knee connected viciously and Fallon uttered a spasmodic grunt of pain. Coldfield uncorked a pair of knee-shaking punches to

Fallon's belly. Fallon could hardly breathe. Now he was pinned against the wall, with Coldfield closing in. The reflected light from the office painted the cruel smile on the saloon owner's lips. Coldfield spread his arms wide, in a catching motion. Fallon leaped to the right, blocked. Then to the left. He was caught. Blocked again, Coldfield moved in.

Fallon ducked, rolled his right shoulder forward and butted Coldfield in the chest, knocking him backwards. Fallon leaped after him, but his foot slipped in the greasy mud and he sprawled forward, his face slamming the wet ground once more. Coldfield whirled, saw his advantage and dropped on both knees on Fallon's back. Fallon's breath exploded from his chest, driven out. Coldfield clubbed Fallon's head deeper into the mud. The thick gluey mud stifled him . . . and suddenly fingers slipped around his throat from behind. Coldfield straddled Fallon's back and his fingers constricted. Fallon's left arm was pinned under him, his right extended. Coldfield had Fallon down so that he could not move, and by leaning forward he could lock his fingers tighter around Fallon's throat. Fallon did not even have the advantage of being able to hit at the strangler's chest, because all Fallon could see was mud, less than an inch from his eyes. Fingers cut, nails bit, and the dark alley grew even darker.

Desperately, Fallon dragged his right arm back and forced it under his own chin. He tried to pry Coldfield's fingers loose. Red pain blinded his eyes. Coldfield held fast, starting a series of squeezes which dug deep into the flesh. Coldfield grunted savagely with effort each time he choked harder. Fallon's hand scrabbled in the mud and came up slimy. In desperation, he tried to smear some of the mud on Coldfield's hand. Coldfield saw what he was up to and automatically released his grip a little to counter Fallon's attack. Too late he realized his mistake. Fallon wrenched the other hand free, stabbed his hands against the treacherous ground, and with a muscle-wracking effort shoved upward. Coldfield cursed dully and toppled off balance, and Fallon was once more on his feet.

Anger stinging him to fury now, Fallon rushed. The prone Coldfield threw up his legs, and his boots caught Fallon in the pit of the belly and heaved, upward and over. Fallon tumbled through the air and crashed against the office wall. Coldfield came after him in a run, head lowered and thrust forward. Turning, Fallon planted his feet hard and unleashed a right a moment before Coldfield tackled him. The whistling right swooped up under Coldfield's outthrust chin and smashed there. Coldfield, his arms flapping, reeled backwards. Like a tiger, Fallon followed him, a tall, lean figure of vengeance, there in the misty gloom of the alley. Both men breathed loudly, and both were covered with black mud. Both, too, were slowly wearing thin, moving groggily, driven by a perverse instinct that said, in spite of pain—fight!

Coldfield's greenish eyes seemed glazed, except for a momentary flash of pure hatred. Strategy had gone. Power alone remained. The two men staggered toward one another. Coldfield threw a punch. Fallon, wearily trying to raise his guard, took the blow in the head. He breathed raggedly, countering Coldfield's next blow, and shot a right of his own. Coldfield's head rolled to the right and his mouth dripped blood between his teeth. A cut over

Fallon's eyebrows dripped redly in his eyes. Fallon felt consciousness slipping away in a black haze. He gouged his upper teeth into his lower lip. The pain, a screaming hurt, tore him awake.

A peculiar silence had descended over the alley. The men stood close, moving very little, each almost ready to topple, each at the end of his physical string. Almost with automatic precision they hit one another. The blows had a thick, crunching sound in the darkness. Each held on. Blood smeared their faces. Fallon's knuckles were torn open and bleeding. A new gash in Coldfield's cheek ran red. Neither would give ground. Each absorbed the terrific punishment of the other's blows, down to the last pain-wracked bone. Fallon's eyesight, blurred periodically, but he held on, smashing, pounding, brutalizing.

Each man waited for the other to fall. . . .

CHAPTER XXI

AN HOUR or two later, Fallon managed to drag himself back to Mrs. Clay's boarding house. There, in the small hours of the night, he heated a kettle of water on the kitchen stove, carried it up to the bathtub and soaked the dirt and blood off his skin. His wounds were either bruises or superficial cuts and gashes, not serious, even though painful. He could only think one thought when he tumbled into bed: I am going to have to kill Mace Coldfield, and it won't be too long now. Thick, dreamless sleep claimed him again.

Rising around noon, he dressed, evaded the curious eyes of the boarders and went out to eat. All day long he received speculative looks from people who wondered what had happened, or knowing ones from people who had also seen Coldfield and thought they knew. The day passed in routine fashion, and he was content to let it do so. Toward evening he began to feel alive again.

Closing the office around midnight, he retired to his

bedroom with a copy of the paper from the state capital. Sprawled out in bed, a cigar in his mouth, the shade drawn, he was reading when it happened.

A roar of shots—five of them, coming in rapid succession—smashed the window and set the blind to dancing. Instantly alert, Fallon dived for cover on the floor. When the shots stopped, he reached up and lifted the lamp from the table. He blew it out, then bellied around the bed, easing his Colt from the holster which hung on the bed post. He kept his head down. Three more shots ripped the night; one of them broke a mirror on the bedroom wall. The other two, fired at a dark target, thudded into the outside wall.

Fallon eased up the blind and peered out. Beyond the veranda rail, he could see nothing. Lifting the curtain all the way, he stepped over the sill onto the veranda, careful not to make any noise on the broken glass that strewed the floor. He held his Colt ready, but still no further shots came. Well, he thought grimly, Coldfield didn't wait long.

Seething with anger, he crouched down, shifted his Colt to his left hand and used his right to feel gingerly along the veranda floor. He collected half a dozen fairly large fragments of broken glass. Standing up again, he moved to the left away from the window. He could make out the silhouette of the house across the alley as his eyes became accustomed to the dark. The bushwhacker, he figured, was hidden there.

He threw the handful of glass toward the window. It tinkled loudly in the still, fragrant night air. Scarcely an instant later, gun flame lanced upward in reddish streaks from the shadows across the alley. The bullets smacked near the window. Fallon, dropping to one knee, slipped his Colt into his right hand and triggered a brace of shots. From the shadows a man screamed hoarsely and fell forward into the alley, clutching his chest and whimpering. Even at a distance, Fallon could see that the man wore a night rider hood. The man uttered harsh, calling noises, and a horse took shape in the gloom also. The downed outlaw caught hold of the stirrup and tried to pull himself into the saddle. The horse danced and whinnied. Fallon heard the wounded man's methodical, bitter cursing.

Not another second to waste. Fallon climbed the veranda rail, lowered himself till he could hang from the veranda floor, and then dropped the rest of the way to the soft earth below. He raced across the lawn as the hooded outlaw got halfway into the saddle. Crashing through bushes, Fallon emerged into the alley just as the outlaw was about to swing his right leg over. Fallon dove through the air, catching that leg and hanging on. The horse reared and screamed. The outlaw, cursing wildly now, clubbed at Fallon's head with his elbow. He succeeded in getting into the saddle, but Fallon reached up and grasped the hood in a tight grip. The outlaw, using his left arm in a cross draw, slapped leather, and Fallon suddenly saw a muzzle staring into his face. With death in his face, he still kept hold of the hood, even as he threw himself backwards. One shot thundered. Acrid powdersmoke stung his nostrils. Hooves rattled on the dusty street, then died, muted in the distance.

Fallon rose to his feet and slapped dust from his clothes. He looked down.

In his hand he held only a feed sack mask.

They had gotten away by inches!

He had to move.

The game was heading into the final hand. He would have only one more chance to get the evidence he needed, and if Coldfield had already silenced Chip Wheeler . . .

He picked up his horse at the livery stable and headed out of Longhorn at a fast gallop.

CHAPTER XXII

POOLS of standing water in the Box W ranch yard reflected the silver and red of late dawn. Water gouted up around the hooves of Fallon's horse as he rode in. He let the horse move at a slow pace, even though time was precious, because he did not want to face Kate. As he tied his horse by the porch, he glanced down to inspect the mud on his boots, and for a second he saw his own mustached face mirrored in the muddy water. A wind he could hardly feel rippled the surface, and the image broke apart like a smashed glass.

He had to get on with it.

Crossing the porch, he heard a bird racket in a nearby bush. No other sound stirred the ranch yard. He rapped on the front door, waited, and rapped again. Finally, when no one answered, he headed round the corner of the house. As he neared the back porch the scent of yeast dough, rich and moist in the morning air, reached his nostrils. His boots smacked loudly on the three rear steps, so that Kate had the door held open when he looked up.

"Eli! What on earth . . ."

Her eyes lit with an unmistakable warmth. The first rays of the sun set her coppery hair on fire. She was wearing a rather plain dress and homemade apron, and her hands were dusted with flour, but for some reason, right at this moment, she looked more attractive to him than ever. He rolled his hat brim under his hands, coughed and said, "Good morning, Kate."

"Well, come in!"

He followed her inside, standing awkwardly. Rising loaves stood on the table, throwing the yeast smell thickly into the air. Kate studied his bruised face with a worried frown. "Eli, what happened to you? Your face . . ."

"Kate," Fallon drew a hard breath, "if it's all the same, we'd best forget about how I look right now. I've got something to say, and it isn't going to be easy." That's the wrong way, his mind cautioned. You've got to play the hand the way you see it. His blue-gray eyes grew harder. "Maybe I'd better talk to Asa about this. Is he around the place somewhere?"

Kate shook her head. "He and the boys rode out early. The storm last night knocked over a tree at our water hole. Lightning did it, they said. Dad's gone out to clear the tree out of the way. The cattle can't get to the water hole as it is. Is the matter really so pressing?" The bright warm spark had cooled somewhat. Her own brow wrinkled in worry as she caught some of Fallon's uneasiness. She came to him hesitantly. "Eli, I don't like to see you like this . . . so bleak."

Raising herself on her toes, she took his face in her hands and pressed her lips fiercely on his. Then she drew back, holding her floured hands awkwardly in front of her.

"Now look what I've done. Honestly, Eli, the things a woman will do . . ."

His smile was only the barest token, a twitch of the lips. Absently he wiped flour from his cheek. "Listen to me, Kate, and try to savvy what I'm going to say. I don't like my own ideas much, but I can't help having them. And there's only one way I can tell them to you, and that's straight."

Puzzled, she did not reply at once. Then with a small moue she moved toward the stove. "Go ahead, then. I'll pour you some coffee."

His sharp gesture stopped her in mid-stride. "No! Let me talk."

She reached forward and gripped the back of a chair as if steadying herself. Clearly, his voice carried a harsher tone than she had been used to in the past weeks.

"All right, Eli."

Another breath. No escaping it now. Fallon looked her in the eye. "Kate, I think Chip may be working for Mace Coldfield."

Emotions flicked across her face like images on a magic lantern screen. First incredulity, deepening to shock, replaced at last by anger. "You're joking with me. You must be joking. You couldn't really mean . . ."

"Yes, I mean it, Kate. I think Chip sold out. I think Chip informed Coldfield that the night riders could trap the cattle at Hawkins' place while most of us were waiting in ambush at Big Creek. I think Chip's to blame—at least partly—for the death of the six men who got killed that night."

"How can you make such an accusation?" she demanded hotly.

"Kate, there's some strong evidence. I'm not saying Chip's sold out for sure. I *think* he has."

"He's my cousin; I know the boy . . ."

"Maybe you don't."

"I don't believe he'd sell my father out."

"You don't believe it because you don't want to. I want to protect Chip because I know he's buzzard meat if Coldfield ever gets on his trail. If Chip will help us for a change, maybe we can settle the trouble in the basin."

"Help us!" Kate's voice rose mockingly. "Speak your own part, why don't you. I thought you had changed a little, but you're still the same. You're bound and determined to carry on this personal war at any cost. You're getting desperate for leads, so you hit out in any direction. . . ."

"That's not true. . . ."

"Isn't it? What else can I think, when you suddenly accuse Chip . . ."

"Why do you keep talking about him like that?" Fallon half-shouted. "Is he some kind of saint?"

Kate grew icy. "He's my flesh and blood."

"And I'm not. Is that what you're trying to tell me?"

"Eli . . ." Her eyes softened the slightest bit.

They faced one another for a long moment. The sunlight spilled stronger into the kitchen now, and the odor of yeast was almost overpowering. Boots slapped suddenly on the back steps. Fallon turned around as Piney Woods limped in the door, a questioning expression in his eyes.

"Hello, Sheriff. Saw your hoss out front . . ."

"Hello, Piney."

Piney's head swung from left to right. He clucked softly. "My! You two look blacker'n the inside of a steer's belly."

"Piney," Fallon asked, "do you know where Chip is?"

Piney pushed his hat back and scratched his chin. "Nope, except that he's gone."

"Gone! He rode out?"

Piney nodded. " 'Bout an hour before dawn. A few minutes before Mr. Wheeler and the rest pulled out. I didn't see it, but Tracy Boone—one of the other hands —saw him go. Chip was really slappin' leather, from what I hear. Tracy said somethin' about it because he wondered why Chip was in such an all-fired hurry."

"Which way was Chip headed? Maybe we can catch him."

"Tracy didn't say, as I recall."

"Where is this Boone now?"

"Out with Mr. Wheeler, workin' on the tree the lightning kicked over into the water hole. Somebody usually has to stay behind to tend the place. Today was my day, so . . ." His words died off as Fallon said:

"Are Chip's things still in the bunkhouse?"

Piney hurried out, returning a minute or so later. He shook his head. "Nope. Bedroll, rifle an' everything cleaned out."

Fallon swung slowly around to face Kate once more. "Is there any reason he might have pulled out without telling anyone? Any reason other than the one I've got in mind?"

146

Piney's brows puckered together. "Not a blamed one. Matter of fact, Mr. Wheeler told him last night at supper that Chip was to stick close to him today. The boss was sort o' riled because Chip hadn't done much work lately, and he aimed to make up for it starting today. One of the hands told Mr. Wheeler that Chip had gone this mornin', before the others were ready to ride out to the water hole, and Mr. Wheeler got madder'n anything. Chip didn't hightail on any ranch business, if that's what you're driving at."

Fallon watched Kate. He could only draw one conclusion from Piney's information: somehow, Chip had gotten wind of Coldfield's plan to wipe him out. Maybe an attack had already been made. At least Chip had been alive when he left the ranch, though that was small consolation.

Kate, her hands whitened into livid knots as she held onto the chair back, stared into an emptiness beyond the table top.

"All right, very well," she repeated tiredly. "I did see Chip this morning."

"Saw him ride out, Miss Kate?" inquired Piney.

She nodded. "I was out of bed an hour before daybreak, out here, working. The dough for this bread takes a long time to rise. I heard a horse come out of the barn. I was standing over there by the window. It was Chip, right enough. I saw him. Does that satisfy you?"

"Not quite," Fallon replied, stung by the barb. "Which way was Chip headed? He could have gone half a dozen different directions."

"The trail up to Halstead?" asked Piney.

"Yes, I think he went in that direction."

"Thanks," Fallon said shortly. "I'm going to head

after him, and see if I can catch up to him before Coldfield does.''

''Sheriff . . .'' Piney spoke.

''What is it?'' Halfway out the door, Fallon stopped.

''You might need an extra gun.''

Fallon frowned. He could not deny the truth of what Piney Woods said. ''All right. Saddle up.'' He left the kitchen, letting the door slam behind him, and walked around to the front of the ranch house with a shaky stride.

CHAPTER XXIII

THE town of North Pass— a collection of slightly more than a dozen wooden buildings, shacks and hovels—lay drowsing sleepily in the moist morning air. The horses of Fallon and Piney Woods threw up geysers of mud and water as the two men raced the mounts past the first outlying shacks. The road—it could hardly be called that, though, for it was only a wide mud belt—cut between the slopes of two hills. Along one side stood the largest building in the settlement, a two-story frame affair. The other ramshackle cabins sprawled up both hillsides. Outside of one of these, a man in blue trousers and a bright red undershirt was shaving in front of a piece of glass hung on the cabin wall to catch the morning light. The man, his face snowy with lather, turned in curiosity as he heard the clatter of the two horses disturb the stillness. Then he went back to his shaving. A cloud crossed the sun. Mud pools in the road flicked dark, then light again.

Fallon pulled up before the large building, which

boasted a sign that read: North Pass General Store and Saloon. Fallon studied the road again as he dismounted. "Not a single blessed footprint. . . ."

"Let's check inside," Piney suggested, although wanly. "Mebbe somebody saw Chip. . . ."

The interior of the store-saloon, cluttered with lanterns hanging from the ceiling, bolts of cloth and a log bar along one wall, smelled of coffee and leather. A man emerged from the back room. "Something I can do fer you gents?" he inquired.

"Have you seen anything of an eighteen- or nineteen-year-old boy this morning?" Fallon asked. "He was probably riding hard. Heading north, for Halstead."

The man scratched at his walrus mustache. "Nope. Ain't seen a living soul since six o'clock this morning, when that cussed . . . uh, the town drunk woke me up a-poundin' on my door for a bottle of likker." Fallon fretted anxiously as the man drawled on: "Wall, I couldn't sleep any more after that, so I figured I'd wash down them windows." He pointed to a pair of glass panes at the store's front. "Right after the rain, y'know. Heck of a lot easier to do it then."

"Have any riders at all gone north through here this morning?" Fallon demanded.

"Not since six-thirty they ain't. I been out in front at the time. (Those windows hadn't been washed down in a year, I'll vow.) I finished up ten, fifteen minutes ago and came back in to unpack a case of goods in the back room." The man screwed his brows into a quizzical frown. "You fellers tailin' somebody? I noticed that badge you're wearing, mister, and . . ."

"Never mind that!" Fallon snapped. "You're sure no youngster has ridden through here?"

"Plumb positive. Now if you two gents would like to sample my likker, I guarantee it's the finest this side of St. Jo, and cheap, too."

But Fallon was already striding out of the store, a bleak expression on his face, Piney on his heels. The two men paused on the sidewalk. "I swear I can't figure it," Piney complained. "Now Miss Kate said that Chip headed north. If he was bent on gettin' out of this territory, the logical place for him to go would be Halstead, and there just ain't no other trail up there, except this one. What do you make of it, Sheriff?"

"I think," said Fallon slowly, "that Miss Kate Wheeler was lying to us."

"Lying! Sheriff, that's pretty strong."

"Come on. We can't waste time palavering. We've already given Coldfield's vultures a couple of more hours to get after Chip."

"Where are we bound for now?" Piney called, following Fallon's example and hastily climbing into his saddle.

"Back to the Box W. . . ."

Piney had no more time to voice his doubts. For Fallon lashed his mount furiously with his spurs, heading out over the trail they had just traveled. Piney galloped in pursuit. As they rode, driving their horses at a gruelling pace, Fallon dared not think what was really in his mind. It was too terrible, too bitter. . . .

CHAPTER XXIV

The sun was an hour down from the high peak of noon when they thundered into the Box W yard. The ranch house door slammed open and Asa Wheeler stalked onto the porch, his eyes angry. "Glad you're here," Fallon said sharply, jumping down from the saddle.

Wheeler, thick thumbs hooked belligerently into his gunbelt, said, "I rode back at noon time from the water hole, wondering where in blazes that Chip was. I told that boy he had to do some honest work today, and here he's still gone."

The door opened again, and Kate, drawn by the sound of loud voices, came out. One glance at her was enough. Fallon could tell that all his suspicions were true. She stood close to the wall in the shadows of the porch, disturbed and even a little frightened.

"Sheriff, have *you* seen that hellion of a nephew of mine?" Wheeler demanded.

"We've been hunting for him. Hasn't your daughter told you?" Acid dripped from Fallon's lips.

"Told me? Told me what?"

"Go on, Kate," Fallon jeered.

"I . . ." She sobbed softly, turned her head to the side and stood with quaking shoulders.

"Tell me *what!*" Wheeler shouted, infuriated. "What is all this? Sheriff, I wish to blazes you'd explain. And, Kate, for the Lord's sake, why are you bawling your head off?"

In the briefest of words Fallon told Wheeler the story of his suspicions, and also what had happened earlier that morning. Wheeler reacted first with disbelief, but then the bitter light of truth penetrated his eyes. "So you see," Fallon finished, "your daughter lied to Piney and me. Chip never went north at all. Chip never was heading for Halstead."

" 'Lying' is pretty strong medicine, Sheriff . . ." Wheeler said, though reluctantly, without much conviction. Hesitantly he faced his daughter. "Kate, does Sheriff Fallon know what he's talking about?"

"Of course I do!" Fallon yelled, unable to control the burning humiliation of disillusionment within him. He stalked onto the porch, seized Kate's shoulders and spun her around. Her face showed confusion; she tried to maintain her anger even as her eyes reddened. "You lied!" Fallon snarled. "Didn't you?"

"All right," she sobbed weakly, writhing in his grip. "Yes, I lied to you."

"Which way did Chip ride, Kate?" Wheeler demanded sternly.

"South."

"This is the truth?"

"Yes, Dad, I swear it is!"

153

"Um." Wheeler grunted thoughtfully. "South . . . sure!" He snapped his fingers. "Sheriff, there's an old cabin in the hills at the south of the basin. Chip and I camped there overnight one time, when I was tryin' to get him interested in hunting. Piney, weren't you along on that trip?"

Piney nodded emphatically. "Yep. That cabin'd be a perfect spot to hide out for a while."

"Would Coldfield or Mitchell know where it is?" Fallon demanded.

"Sure," Wheeler replied, "Lots of the boys around here use it, though it's pretty well run down. Huntin's good down there."

"But would Coldfield think to look for Chip there?" Fallon demanded.

"No-o-o," Wheeler drawled, speculating.

". . . but Chip sure as the devil doesn't know anything about covering a trail," Piney interjected. "If they were following him . . ."

"Piney, we're riding for that cabin!" Fallon said quickly. "Asa, where are your boys?"

"Why, still at the water hole, haulin' on that tree . . ."

"Ride out and get them. And then follow us to that cabin. I've got a feeling that we may need plenty of help, if Coldfield or some of his bunch haven't cashed in the boy's hand for good."

No seconds were wasted. Fallon, Piney and Wheeler mounted up. As Fallon wheeled his mount, he caught a last glimpse of Kate standing stiffly on the porch, one hand against the support post. She wavered unsteadily on her feet, her eyes filled with pain. Fallon cursed to himself and roweled his horse viciously. With a shout, Wheeler cut out of the ranch yard and off up a rise toward the water hole. Piney called directions which Fallon hardly heard. They hit the south trail three quarters of a mile from the Box W, and the tracks of a single horse were plain in the drying mud. Fallon and Piney exchanged silent glances.

"The fool kid!" Piney exclaimed. "Didn't even have sense enough to cover his trail."

A few hours later they started to climb the foothills, riding slowly and carefully now, hands near their guns. Boulders threw immense black shadows and the sun burned a fierce furnace-red in the western skies. A bird took wing from a stunted tree and the flap of its wings startled Fallon, who streaked for his Colt, then checked himself. Piney's face twisted; you could not have called it a smile.

The jagged hillsides grew darker and a bluish gloom began to settle. Suddenly, Piney held up one hand. Both horses stopped dead still. Silence hung across the sky and the hills.

Somewhere ahead, Fallon could hear the racket of gunshots, cracking out one after another. They dismounted and climbed on foot, moving around boulders, scouting the way ahead. Abruptly they emerged from behind one mammoth slab of rock, and six yards ahead Fallon saw a hooded figure squatting on guard in the gloom. The night rider saw Piney and Fallon at the same instant. With a sharp cry of surprise, he leaped to his feet, fumbling to unholster his Colt. Fallon did not want to risk gunfire. He snatched up a rock and lobbed it hard, before the outlaw could shoot. The jagged rock struck the outlaw's skull and the man toppled. He pitched forward down a steep slope, rolling over and over, while his gun lay glittering blue in the fading light scant feet from where Fallon stood.

Fallon watched the masked figure tumble and roll away far down the slope in a cloud of dust. He started down after the man, wanting to tear the mask off. Then he heard the gunfire up ahead again, caught the warning in Piney's eyes and nodded tightly. They would have to unmask another one. They had to keep going.

They pressed forward, Colts ready in their hands now. Only the distant peaks of the hills remained bathed in a reddish radiance. Like twin shadows they slipped up another gully as the sound of firing grew louder. Piney moved with surprising agility for one lame, though the effort showed on the dirty mask of sweat glistening on his game little face. They slid along the gully wall. The wind carried a smell of powdersmoke.

"Right up beyond that brush," Piney indicated. "There's sort of a little cup of a valley, with the cabin right smack in the bottom."

Crawling over the sharp stones, they pushed into the brush and found themselves bellied down on the rim of the circular slope that ran all the way around the tiny natural valley. The cabin, its walls caved in in several places, its windows empty of glass, sat below them. All around the slope Fallon saw figures crouched in the gloom: hooded figures. Puffs of smoke bloomed whitely. Rifles and pistols cracked. Shots thugged into the cabin below. And minutes apart came answering shots from the cabin.

"He's still alive in there . . ." Piney breathed.

Fortunately, there was ample cover in the form of brush

and rocks all over the slopes of the little valley. The night riders could hide easily, but it also might be possible for Fallon and Piney to slip down to the cabin unobserved, to add their guns to that of the boy. Fallon figured there were a dozen night riders here. Somehow, he and Piney had to even the odds and bring Chip Wheeler out alive. . . .

The firing slacked off for a moment or two, giving Fallon the opportunity carefully to survey the situation. Twilight was fast deepening; already the hollow where the cabin stood swam in murky blue shadow. Brush around the valley wall assumed a black hue, and the only real light shone high up, where the last rays of the sun coated gold the belly of the sky. From his left, Fallon heard a voice cry out, muffled and indistinct: "The kid can't hold out much longer."

This, Fallon knew grimly, was true. With his eyes he mapped a course down the treacherous hillside. He tapped Piney's shoulder and re-traced the route again in pantomime. Piney nodded. "We've got to reach Chip before one of their bullets gets him," Fallon clipped out. "We'll try it quiet as we can. Then, if they spot us, run for the cabin." He hurried on, the old tightness within him. "If one of us gets killed . . . the other's got to bring the boy out alive, or hold on until help arrives."

"I know that," Piney replied. Both men thought of death mechanically; they had to treat it as a vague, unreal thing, because every bit of their energy had to be concentrated on the task ahead. As they lay gazing out through the brush over the rim, Piney whispered, "Ready any time you give the word."

Fallon glided to his feet, staying in a half-crouch.

Hoarse orders were being called out between the outlaws strung around the basin rim. A rifle cracked and a shingle on the cabin roof flew high. Answering spurts of flame gouted from a shadowy window of the cabin. Fallon and Piney had two dozen yards to run downhill before they reached good cover; then boulders and brush would screen them until they were twenty yards from the cabin. Risky. They would be clear targets, even in the half-light, while in the open. Their safety depended upon heads being turned toward the cabin. Otherwise . . .

Fallon checked that thought.

Time to move. Rifles and pistols slammed from all sides of the tiny valley. They half ran, half slid down the shaly hillside for several yards while the crack and buzz of shots tore the brush nearby. Slightly to their left along the rim, a night rider had been posted with a Winchester; before they started their headlong plunge, Fallon had momentarily glimpsed its muzzle protruding over the rim edge. Now suddenly, with the covering boulders and brush still a few seconds away, the night rider nearest them ripped out with a startled oath that Fallon heard clearly. He knew what was coming, even as he stopped his frantic run and felt his calf muscles quiver while stiff legs braced him to a halt. Piney plummeted on by, the force of his run carrying him nearer cover as the Winchester barked twice. The bullets kicked up spurts of shale. Fallon, spinning around, blasted two matching shots at the night rider. A startled silence hung over the valley for an instant. The brush where Fallon had fired rattled and crashed; the night rider jerked to his feet as if burned with a hot iron. He threw the Winchester to his shoulder once more—

—And then he dropped it, seizing his stomach. He screamed hoarsely and pitched forward over the rim, screaming and kicking as he rolled downward in a cloud of rising dust. The whole incident had lasted a tenth of the time it takes to tell, and Fallon had already dived for the protective cover a few yards below. The other night riders evidently realized they had more than one man against them, because as Fallon and Piney catfooted on down the slope, screened now, slugs chewed the earth and boulders behind them.

Another half-minute brought them to the fringe of cover, with the shadowy cabin only a scant distance away. Piney scouted briefly to the right, and returned with a report: "Back door looks like the best way in. Some fair cover." Fallon nodded, made an imperative gesture with his Colt barrel, and Piney led off in the direction of the rear of the cabin. They crouched low in the brush for a moment; they would have to run across open ground again. But here, the shadows blanketed all with thickening bluish darkness. The night riders would now have a difficult time finding clear targets. So after a moment's pause, Fallon darted out and made it safely to the cabin door, which he kicked open.

He halted only a split second within the cabin door.

At the sudden crash of sound from Fallon's entrance, Chip Wheeler, crouched by a lightless window on his knees, spun around, his pale blue eyes flaring with a startled animal's fright. He aimed at Fallon automatically. As Fallon leaped, he had a grisly and vivid picture of the boy's pale face, and his knuckles whitening on the trigger in the gloom.

Fallon batted the Colt barrel down. The shot boomed

and racketed in the narrow confines of the cabin. The slug plowed a furrow in the dirt. The closing door, with Piney leaning against it uttering a relieved sigh, gave the final coda of sound.

Outside, stillness. Then Fallon heard the raspy whine of Chip Wheeler's breathing.

"I didn't know who . . ." he began thinly.

"Save it," Fallon replied. "We're in a tight." He noticed a row of shells laid out on the dirt floor in front of Chip. Fallon pointed to them. "Those your last?"

Chip gulped, nodded. The befuddled expression passed from his pale eyes, and he seized Fallon's arm with thin, desperate fingers. "Listen . . ." he said, his voice ragged, close to a sob. "You've got to help me, Sheriff. Those men out there . . . they want to *kill* me!" The stressed word had a reedy quality, as if the boy could not believe what he knew to be true.

Piney's foot made noise as the bantam-sized puncher dragged himself to a position beside the window. He peered out. "They're pretty quiet . . ." he mused. "Must be figuring to close in."

"Help me, for God's sake!" Chip protested.

The cabin interior lay muffled in dusty-smelling shadows. In one corner a spider crawled down the leg of an overturned table. Fallon stared hard at the weak-faced boy. "We'll help you, provided you do a little talking when we get out of here."

The boy reeled to his feet, flushing. "We've got to get out!" he shouted hysterically. "We've . . ."

Crack! Crack!

Fallon hit Chip's knees and dragged him to the floor

again as slugs whined through the window and chunked against the wall opposite. Piney drew a bead, fired, then followed up with two more shots. A thin yelp drifted down the slope. Piney grunted, the corners of his mouth lifting slightly. Fallon glanced at the panting youth who lay propped on one elbow.

"Yes, I did!" Chip exclaimed, nodding fiercely. "I did it. I wanted to get out of the Basin. Coldfield paid me good money, but now he's trying to kill me." Again the boy clutched Fallon. "I played it square with him! Then last night two of his men shot at me when I was riding back to the ranch. I *had* to clear out. I didn't know where else to go except here. I knew they'd look for me in Halstead." The boy jammed his palms against his eyes and sobbed. His voice had a pitifully young sound. "Why do they want to kill me now? Why? Why?"

Fallon and Piney exchanged grim looks. Fallon knew he had his evidence.

"Sheriff . . ." Piney's warning whisper and sharp gesture brought Fallon to attention. High up, Fallon could see a red wash in the sky, but the valley slope was dark. Yet Fallon was able to make out moving patches of shadow, blackest black of all on that hillside. "Appears to me," Piney said softly, "that the circle is closing."

Fallon nodded. Help should be on its way. Asa Wheeler and his men could not have been too far behind them.

Retrieving Chip Wheeler's fallen Colt, the sheriff thrust it into the boy's hand. He pushed Chip roughly to the window. "Don't expect us to do all the shooting. You're in this just as deep as Piney or me. Now come on!" Fallon snarled. He slapped the boy hard across the face. "Settle

161

down and stop that sniveling or none of us will get out of here alive."

Chip fingered the Colt butt, controlling his sobs. "What are you going to do?"

"I'm going out and catch one of them," Fallon said quietly. "And this time, I aim to hold on to the one I catch. Piney, can you handle things here? I'm going to hide up in the brush a little way, and wait till they close in. Give me mebbe half a minute, and then cut loose. I'll keep down."

"Right," Piney nodded.

Fallon eased out the back door, crouched down and sidled along the wall to the front of the cabin. He too could hear the night riders advancing on foot down the slope. They rattled through the brush, even talked loudly among themselves. Nearly a dozen, Fallon had estimated when first he and Piney had arrived on the scene. They were confident, all right. A dozen or more guns against three. If Asa Wheeler didn't show . . .

Above him on the slope, Fallon could make out the shadowy silhouette of one of the night riders. Some trick of light, some sudden cast of starshine, must have alerted the night rider that another person lurked in the shadows close at hand. For the man stopped, then called softly, "Hey! Hey, Rio! Is that you down there? You're supposed to be over farther the other way."

With the sound of the whispered words masking the noise of his movement, Fallon slipped up the hillside. The night rider hesitated, then laughed nervously. "Come on, Rio, quit fooling! We haven't got time for any of your stunts." The man's laughter was a thin, piping whinny of a sound. Fallon paused an instant, smiling grimly. He knew that laugh. He had heard it his first night in town, when he'd shot Mitchell's hand, Bleeker. This man's name was Simms. Another of Luke Mitchell's gunnies. Fallon felt as if an icy splash of cold water had struck him. Here at last was real proof—a night rider he could identify.

Fallon threw caution aside and raced across the intervening ground. "Wha . . . !" Simms cursed thickly and threw up his gun. He fired; the night bloomed with a red flame flower. Fallon hit the dirt as the bullet chunked and screamed off a boulder. Fallon's own gun answered, speaking at the target limned against the high, pale starlight. Simms uttered a choking sound, danced a few steps in the shale, and toppled. Fallon raced forward to the fallen body and ripped the feed sack mask away. But before he had time to look closely at the white blur of the dead outlaw's face, other shots rang out. They sent him ducking for cover again, as night riders converged on both sides to investigate Simms' cry, which evidently had carried a good distance. Fallon slid in behind a rock, waited, fired at a gunflash and heard a howl of pain.

Then, blending with the rising crescendo of gunfire, a new voice thrust raggedly through the darkness, shouting its hoarse warning: "Hightail! Ranchers, git to the horses! Move!" In the next few seconds a number of different impressions struck Fallon's senses: the fire of the night riders dropped off to a few sporadic shots; men crashed loudly through the brush, apparently heading toward the opposite side of the tiny valley; other voices echoed and roared from the valley rim behind Fallon. Recognizing them, he called:

163

"Wheeler! Wheeler! Down this way."

More men pelted down the slope, guns ready. But the night riders had melted away swiftly, undoubtedly not prepared to cope with more than two or three adversaries. *Coldfield is still playing it close.* Fallon thought with bitter satisfaction as he saw Asa Wheeler come lumbering down the slope toward him.

CHAPTER XXV

"LOOK HERE—all of you!" Fallon raised his voice. The cowhands converged. "Strike a light, Asa. I've got something to show you."

The match scraped on a rock and bloomed with an odor of sulphur. One of the men caught his breath sharply. The dancing flame showed a gory picture on the ground: Simms, the Mitchell rider, lay twisted in a grotesque pose, his mouth open, his eyes glazed.

"Recognize him, Asa?"

"Yes, o'course I do."

"Mitchell man," said one of the hands.

"Name of Simms," chimed in another.

"Is that proof enough?" Fallon asked. "Does that show you who the night riders really are?"

Wheeler drew a deep breath. "Yeah, I reckon it does."

"I reckon," spoke another voice in the dark, "it's time we fight."

"Can't do much else," a third voice announced.

"Looks to me like this whole range war has suddenly come smack out in the open."

Fallon was about to speak, about to tell the small group of hands of Chip's evidence, but was prevented from doing this by the abrupt appearance of a figure from the shadows. A foot scraped audibly on the ground. "It's me, Sheriff—Piney." The bantam-sized puncher joined the circle gathered around the corpse.

"Piney!" Wheeler exclaimed, remembering. "Is Chip down in that cabin?"

"That's what I came to tell you," Piney replied somberly. "A couple of minutes before the fighting stopped . . . well, one of the slugs got him."

"How bad is he hurt?" Fallon asked sharply.

"Pretty bad, looks to me like. He's about half out of his head. I think we better get him back to the ranch."

Wheeler issued rapid orders. A man was sent to fetch horses. Two others gathered up the body of Simms for transportation back to the Box W.

Doc Overmill from Longhorn awaited them at the Box W ranch, but within the hour Chip Wheeler had died.

CHAPTER XXVI

BUCK KIMSON happened to be the first Rocking L hand awake the following morning. He couldn't stay asleep; after that raid on the hill cabin the night before turned out wrong, he had had a feeling that things were not going to run so smoothly from now on.

He got out of bed, pulled his galluses up over his shoulders, scratched his coarse beard, picked up his razor and whetstone and let himself out the back door of the bunkhouse. He shaved off the stubble, returned to the bunkhouse, slipped on shirt, hat and gun belt, and then, with makings in his hand, ambled out the front door of the bunkhouse into the ranch yard.

The gate faced east, and over the hills yonder Buck

could see a long bloody smear of light on the horizon, like a bullet wound. He blinked, drew in a lungful of the cool morning air and started to roll a cigarette. Then his eyes chanced to light on the high cross bar over the gate. His mouth went slack and he dropped the tobacco sack. He turned and started to yell. He kept on yelling as he charged across the ranch house porch and started beating on the door. What he had seen hanging from the gate cross bar turned his stomach weak.

It was Simms. The Mitchell crew had not missed him until they were well away from the hills the night before. Simms had a rope around his neck, and the rope hung from the cross bar. Simms' body turned slightly in the morning breeze, showing the bullet holes someone had pumped into him. Buck Kimson pounded all the louder on the door. At last the door opened. Luke Mitchell towered there, powerful and rangy. His small dark eyes were drunken, but he sobered instantly when he saw the hanging corpse. He cursed steadily for several seconds. His stubbled chin, disheveled hair and reeking breath made him a horrible scarecrow figure in the bloody morning light.

"You know what that means, Buck?" Mitchell said savagely. "It means we're fighting the ranchers in the open, starting right now. I expect that's some of Fallon's work, and he wouldn't't've done it if he didn't have plenty guns behind him. Saddle your horse, Buck. Ride to Longhorn." Mitchell's eyes gave off the evil glare of a cornered beast.

"Git Coldfield out here," Mitchell said. "Pronto! Or we'll all be swinging."

Buck Kimson ran for his horse. Seconds later he thundered out of the Rocking L ranch yard. He had to duck as he swept under the gate, to avoid the dangling heels of the corpse with the hangnoose around its neck.

CHAPTER XXVII

THE SUN beat down on Longhorn.

A few minutes past noon; the streets silent, deserted; the muted thunder of a thousand head, moving sluggishly along the streets, through the town, toward the cattle pens; Fallon and Asa Wheeler on point, Fallon high in the saddle, hawk's eyes wary, a tight knot of clod in his stomach. They had pushed out at dawn, two dozen armed ranchers. They had taken the open trail and seen no sign of Mitchell, Coldfield and the other outlaws. Now the herd plodded toward the shipping pens, and Fallon rode slowly. The sun burned with ominous heat. The dust rose in fantastic, swirling clouds, choking the nostrils and clogging the throat. The herd strung out between the buildings. Not a soul stirred on the street. Not one. Word had gotten around. Showdown.

Fallon noticed that they were just passing Mace Coldfield's house. He saw a blur of white in an upper window, and peered more closely through the screen of dust. He made out India Coldfield, standing behind the glass, holding the drapery aside. Her mouth hung open, and ugly bruises showed on her face, neck and arms. She watched, like a demented child, as the herd passed, and though Fallon could hear no sound, it looked to him as though she were laughing idiotically behind the window. Sickened, he turned away.

Had Coldfield run out without a fight? Somehow, that didn't seem believable. After all, the man had a stake in his outlaw business. He could no longer make the business profitable, but Fallon felt that Coldfield would at least want to take revenge; men of his stamp always did. And that was what Fallon anticipated.

The herd pushed on through the main street. Here a few spectators, bolstered by liquor, lined the sidewalks to gawk. The Crystal was shut down tight. Asa Wheeler shook his head as they rode. "They should have hit us by now. Where in the name o' sense are they? I don't like this one bit."

"Neither do I," Fallon admitted truthfully.

Down by the tracks, they herded the cattle into pens. They climbed off their horses and perched on the fences. Winchester barrels shone blue in the late noon light. Fallon smoked one cigar after another. The town burned and simmered in a heat haze. The men grew nervous. The minutes ticked off. At four-thirty a train would come out from the yards on the run to the capital, and they would load the stock aboard. Until then . . .

"Listen!" Wheeler caught Fallon's arm savagely. "Riders."

But it was only one, coming at a gallop. "It's Tom

Nash!'' Fallon exclaimed. He leaped down from the corral rail and stamped his cigar into the dust. Nash, disheveled, threw himself off his horse and rushed forward.

"For God's sake, Fallon!" Nash cried. "Pete Hookens just staggered into my place."

"Hookens? Who the blazes is he?"

"Engineer," Nash gasped. "Railroad . . . he was getting up a head of steam on a locomotive in the yards . . . and Coldfield and his bunch rode in and took over a whole blasted train; shot Pete in the hip. He came to me because my place is the only one left open."

"When was this?" Fallon snapped.

"Ten, fifteen minutes ago."

The other ranchers had gathered around in a tight group. Panic seized Fallon. With gall and daring, Coldfield, Mitchell and their bunch could seize an entire train and run it down here by the pens. That meant . . . Fallon cursed. Gunfire would drive the penned cattle wild. The confusion would help Coldfield not a little.

The death's head expression sat on Fallon's face again. Slowly he extracted his Colt and checked it.

The snorting and bawling of the cattle in the pens suddenly had an ominous sound. The other ranchers had realized the new danger; they knew only too well that a couple of dozen armed men could easily overpower the skeleton crews kept at the railroad yards.

Fallon leaped to the fence and stood high, searching the track as it cut between buildings toward the other side of town. The rails gleamed hotly in the sun. The cattle milled and pushed restlessly, and all too suddenly the pens appeared flimsy. Then, far down the track, Fallon saw a white plume of smoke mount the glare of the sky.

Then, with a shriek, the distant engine whistle shrilled the challenge to battle.

A moment of grim silence hung over the tracks and the shipping pens. Even the cattle seemed to cease their restless bawling. Fallon gazed over the group: Asa Wheeler, stout, his hair gray, his face drawn in a tight frown as he held a pair of heavy Colts in his hands; Lucius Field, the tall hawkish man with the flinty gaze, hefting a Winchester almost tenderly while his mouth tightened in a thin, determined line; Piney Woods, a small man compared to the rest of the ranchers, yet standing erect with his shoulders thrown back and a determined expression on his face that matched Field's. Fallon felt the old, tight chill in his belly that always came before a fight. This fight promised to be the toughest in which he had ever wielded his gun. But he was ready. Like the other ranchers, he could not completely keep from being scared; it was not an easy thing to face the guns of hired killers, even when driven by the kind of a desire for vengeance that burned within Fallon. He would not back down, though. The fact was, he could not back down now even if he desired.

For the plume of smoke climbed the sky, the rails vibrated, and now Fallon could even make out the pair of stag antlers mounted on the engine's storm lantern. There was a single flatcar hooked behind the tender, and riding this were Mitchell, Coldfield and the outlaws. The thunder of the approaching train grew louder. Two blocks away now. Fallon shouted: "Mount up! They'll be on foot."

The ranchers clambered into the saddle, waiting. Piney caught Fallon's eye and grinned.

"Luck, Sheriff!" he called.

Fallon's face remained bleak. The engine slowed, its ponderous drivers thundering, and the outlaws began to pile off down the line of pens. Guns barked and acrid puffs of blue smoke floated over the pens. The ranchers galloped down the narrow roadway between track and pens, while cattle began to bawl and stamp, and here and there a steer threw himself against the side of the pen, eyes rolling frantically.

The engine had stopped completely, and the outlaw at the throttle had already been picked off by Lucius Field. The ranchers tangled with the "night riders"—who no longer wore masks—and the sound of gunfire rocked the town. The fight became a tangled melee of screaming, plunging, horses, smoke and shooting. Fallon aimed, fired, and saw an outlaw go down. Another ran toward him, clutching at his stirrups and raising his Colt to blast Fallon's head at point-blank range. Fallon threw his head down just as the outlaw's gun exploded, and the slug ripped over his head. Whipping his arm down, Fallon fired an answering shot. Less than eight inches from the gun's muzzle, the outlaw's face dissolved into bloody ruin.

Through the smoke-blue confusion, Fallon searched for Coldfield, did not see him. He caught sight of Mitchell on the opposite side of the fighting. Mitchell had spotted him too, and was desperately trying to reach Fallon, a hateful expression on his stubbled face. As Fallon watched, Mitchell shot at Lucius Field, and the tall rancher toppled from the saddle, his jaw blown half away. Fallon felt his stomach twist and writhe. Across the throng, Mitchell's face split into a vicious grin as he vaulted into Field's empty saddle and fought his way toward the sheriff, firing as he came.

Fallon surveyed the scene quickly. After only a few moments of fighting, it was painfully apparent that the battle would be short, for the ranchers were no match for professional gun hands. They were dropping right and left, killed or wounded; the rancher force was nearly cut in half already, while most of the outlaws still remained in operation. The outlaws too had taken to horseback as Mitchell had done. A man on a horse had an advantage of height from which to shoot. In another short space, Fallon realized, the battle would end in defeat for the ranchers. . . .

Their only chance for victory was to outnumber the outlaws, and Fallon could not see how the ranchers could succeed in doing that.

With a thunderous crash, one of the pens buckled and a knot of bawling, frantic steers poured forth into the dust. Tossing horns caught a rancher and threw him high as he screamed. Fallon hurriedly reloaded his Colt, just as something hard caught him in the left shoulder. The impact knocked him from the saddle and he twisted as he hit the ground. Over him towered Luke Mitchell, mounted, a sadistic grin on his face that showed only one desire: murder. Mitchell sawed back on his mount's reins. Only by a quick roll did Fallon avoid the slashing hooves of the animal as they split the dirt. Desperately Fallon brought his gun up and fired.

Mitchell's jaw dropped. He swayed in the saddle, and the ragged hole in his throat gouted blood as he fell to the ground.

Fallon scrambled to his feet, fighting the pain that washed over him. He looked wildly for Coldfield, and finally spotted him. The ex-saloon owner was crouched in the locomotive cab, a Winchester in his hands, watching the battle with a speculative expression in his greenish eyes. Fallon felt hatred mount in his chest again. Insanely, he kicked a rancher out of the way and bolted for the tracks. He passed Asa Wheeler, who shouted:

"Sheriff, we got to have some help!"

Fallon ignored him, pushing on. Coldfield stood upright in the cab now, some six feet above Fallon and a good eight feet away. He saw Fallon coming, and a vicious hardness etched itself around his mouth. Through a ragged cloud of powdersmoke, the Winchester barrel gleamed. Fallon's shoulder throbbed, but he pushed through the last knot of fighting men. Red pain swam behind his eyes, threatening unconsciousness. He threw another man out of the way, but in doing so, he lost his balance. His mind cursed frantically. He felt his legs dissolving beneath him. He tried to regain balance and merely succeeded in landing flat on his back.

Above him, in the engine cab, taking the opportunity that had suddenly come in such a short space of seconds, Mace Coldfield smiled cruelly, raised the Winchester and aimed it at Fallon's chest. Fallon, unable to move for one crimson instant, lay blinking dazedly.

Coldfield's finger whitened on the trigger.

Fallon's mind cried a warning. He struggled to move, feebly brought his gun up. . . .

Suddenly a shadow crossed between Fallon and Coldfield, moving with a limping run into the breech.

Simultaneously, the Winchester cracked.

Dazed, not believing his eyes, Fallon saw Piney Woods stiffen as the shot drilled him clean through the chest. Even as Fallon fired in the next instant, his mind seemed detached, floating a hundred miles away in space.

Fallon's shot rang out loudly.

The rifle dropped from Coldfield's hands, and the ex-saloon owner went to his knees, his lips writhing with obscene curses. He clutched at his chest, trying to stanch the sticky flow of redness widening on his shirt bosom. Then he slid forward on the locomotive cab platform and his eyes went closed. His cheek rested against the platform. A fold of cheek flesh was pushed up under Coldfield's eye in a way which made the dead man look utterly horrible.

Fallon climbed to his feet. A bawling steer raged past, and Fallon staggered out of the way just in time. Lying belly down in the dirt, Piney Woods had his eyes open, and his gaze locked with Fallon's for a moment. It was as though Piney had been clinging to life until he could get Fallon to look at him. Fallon knelt down beside the bantam-sized puncher. Dust stung Fallon's eyes and caked on his tongue as he tried to speak to the dying cowboy.

Piney's lips moved. "Had to pay you back some way. . . ." The puncher stiffened. Fallon turned his head away, suddenly tortured by doubt and indecision. Then, abruptly, he remembered the battle. It raged on, down the track a short distance. Fallon stumbled to his feet and blinked once more. For in the midst of the fray he spotted Tom Nash, wielding a pair of six-guns. Moreover, the ranchers had been reinforced by a dozen new men. It took Fallon a moment to recognize them: Flanders, who owned the grain and feed store; Roke, the hardware store owner; Peters, from the livery stable . . . all of them merchants or saloon keepers in Longhorn. The outlaws, both their leaders gone, were being driven back and surrounded. The ranchers with their new recruits were winning, and one by one, the outlaws threw down their guns.

Fallon stood weaving on his feet in the bright sunlight. Another steer trotted past. The bawling of others rose from the pens. A last shot cracked the air. Dust clouded around Fallon's head, and silence settled. Then he saw Asa Wheeler running toward him. He shook his head, unable to think because of the pain in his shoulders. Wheeler was grinning and shouting at him, but Fallon could not understand the words.

Got to move . . . Fallon thought.

He took one step forward . . . and keeled over on his face.

CHAPTER XXVIII

ROLLING the cigar in his hand, Fallon shook his head. "I still can't believe it."

Across from him, Tom Nash smiled and shrugged. They were seated in the sheriff's office. It was the day following the battle. Fallon's arm was bound up in a cloth sling.

"What's so difficult to understand, Sheriff?" Nash asked.

"The reason why you suddenly turned up yesterday, when things were going against us."

Nash waved deprecatingly. "Not so difficult, Sheriff. I saw how the fight was going, so I rounded up a dozen men here on the street and pitched in."

Still unable to believe what he now had to believe, Fallon said fervently, "But why? It wasn't your fight."

"Wasn't it? After all, you're the sheriff of Longhorn, but we couldn't expect you to carry the whole weight by yourself. Keeping a town clean isn't the job for one man

179

alone. And if you're wondering why *I* suddenly became inspired to join the conflict, I'll remind you that I once promised to repay the favor you did me by quieting down the bully boys who used to wreck my place every other night.''

Fallon gazed thoughtfully at the smoke curling up blue from his cigar. Pleasant sunlight fell warmly through the window. In the back of the office, he could hear the sullen conversation of the outlaws who had been left alive at the battle's end. The cells were filled to capacity.

''By the way,'' Nash spoke up, ''I saw India Coldfield leave Longhorn on the morning train.'' Nash's eyes grew somber for a moment. ''I'm afraid she's losing her mind. Perhaps she'll be able to regain her balance if she returns to the East. As for me, I rather think Longhorn will be a garden spot of the West, now that the night riders are definitely out of business.''

''Nash . . .''

''Yes?''

''You heard what Piney Woods did for me?''

Nash nodded.

''I never would have believed a man would lay down his life like that,'' Fallon said helplessly.

Nash smiled gayly, though his humor could not conceal the seriousness of his thought. ''Sheriff, there are men in this world like Mace Coldfield, but there are also men like Piney, and it's a fortunate thing that the Pineys out-number the Coldfields. Else I would pack up my Gladstone, beat a retreat into the wilderness and quietly slit my throat.''

Shortly after that, Nash left the office, and Fallon sat

smoking a while longer. His whole scale of values had shifted again; he felt bitter remorse when he recalled how he had once been ready to accuse Piney of being "grateful" so that he could call the sheriff his friend. The thought of that made Fallon ashamed. The shadow across the sun, the figure that shambled between Fallon and Coldfield's Winchester muzzle, had paradoxically lifted a cloud from Fallon's mind. Now, for the first time, he actually believed he could see things clearly and true.

The unselfishness of Tom Nash, and especially of Piney Woods, even made it possible for him to see Kate's behavior in a new light.

Kate. . . .

Fallon bolted out of his chair, wincing as he was reminded of his wound. But he had delayed too long already, out of stubborn pride. In another moment he was in the saddle and riding toward the Box W.

They rode out from the ranch, Kate and Fallon, moving slowly. She had made no reply when he arrived at the ranch and asked if he could talk with her; only nodded. Asa Wheeler on the porch had beamed with a pleasure he could not conceal. And Fallon, catching sight of her coppery hair and gray eyes, had called himself a fool for ever thinking he could get her out of his blood.

The sun threw warm highlights in her hair as they rode. At last he cleared his throat hesitantly.

"Kate . . ."

"Eli, please, let me speak first. I don't blame you for feeling betrayed. I realize how selfishly I acted." She smiled a hesitant smile. "It only took me a few moments

181

to realize just how shabby my behavior really was. You had every right to think me a hypocrite. I can only say I'm sorry.'' She looked away. Her voice became very quiet. ''I beg . . .''

''No!'' He reached across and took her hand. ''I've learned a lot in these last two days, Kate. I've been plenty wrong too. So maybe we can wipe the slate clean and start again.''

Fiercely she pressed his hand. ''Yes, Eli, we can!''

He smiled. ''Y'know, I never liked that name Eli. But now it sounds good to me. I've still got some time to put in as a lawman, but I think Eli'd be a good name for a rancher, too.'' He gazed deeply into her eyes and saw the promise of peace there. He grew serious for a moment. ''When we bury Piney, we'll bury Reb Fallon too.''

She nodded, and he thought her eyes glistened with tears, but he could not be sure.

They rode on across the basin in the morning sun. . . .

> He'll be hanging up his gun,
> He'll be hanging up his gun. . . .
> And with a woman by his side,
> His killing days are done,
>
> Say farewell!
> Say farewell!
> To the man with the fast, fast gun. . . .

EASY TO READ ★ LARGE TYPE

The Best from the West!

70820 Rawhiders of the Brasade Foreman $1.25

71010 Rebel Town Zavada $1.50

82085 Track of the Killer Moore 95¢

82380 Trail for Tennihan Lawrence $1.50

86140 The Vengeance Seeker #1 Knott 95¢

86141 The Vengeance Seeker #2 Knott 95¢

---

*86142 **The Vengeance Seeker** #3 Knott $1.25

---

*87261 **The War On Charity Ross** Bickham 95¢

Available wherever paperbacks are sold or use this coupon.

🍎 **ace books,** (Dept. MM) Box 576, Times Square Station New York, N.Y. 10036

Please send me titles checked above.

⊩ enclose $. . . . . Add 35c handling fee per copy.

Name . . . .

Address . . . .

City. . . . . State. . . . . Zip. . . . .

9K

L.P. HOLMES

31731	**The Hardest Man In the Sierras** 95¢
52241	**The Maverick Star** 95¢
70880	**Rawhide Creek** 95¢
75081	**The Savage Hours** 75¢
76335	**Side Me At Sundown** 95¢
89591	**Wolf Brand/Buzzards of Rocky Pass** $1.25

L.L. FOREMAN

Just 95c each

47201	**Last Stand Mesa**
54721	**The Mustang Trail**
ᴏ7131	**The Plundering Gun**
*73436	**Rogues Legacy**
*76591	**The Silver Flame**
77770	**Spanish Grant**

Available wherever paperbacks are sold or use this coupon.

🅐 **ace books,** (Dept. MM) Box 576, Times Square Station New York, N.Y. 10036

Please send me titles checked above.

I enclose $................. Add 35c handling fee per copy.

Name ....

Address ....

City.................... State............. Zip........

8H

Winner of the **SPUR AWARD** for Best Western novel

08381	**The Buffalo Runners**	Grove	75¢
10230	**Sam Chance**	Capps	$1.25
*13905	**The Day the Cowboys Quit** Kelton		$1.25
29741	**Gold In California**	Ballard	$1.25
34270	**The Honyocker**	Lutz	$1.50
47081	**The Last Days of Wolf Garnett** Adams		$1.25
48919	**The Long Run**	Nye	75¢
*55122	**My Brother John**	Purdum	$1.25
77152	**The Red Sabbath**	Patten	$1.25
*80270	**The Time It Never Rained** Kelton		$1.25
82090	**Tragg's Choice**	Adams	75¢
*82135	**The Trail to Ogallala**	Capps	$1.25
85902	**The Valdez Horses**	Hoffman	75¢
88562	**White Man's Road**	Capps	$1.25

Available wherever paperbacks are sold or use this coupon.

ace books, (Dept. MM) Box 576. Times Square Station New York. N.Y. 10036
Please send me titles checked above.

I enclose $. . . . . Add 35c handling fee per copy.

Name . . . .

Address . . . .

City. . . . . State. . . . . Zip. . . . .

12G

Ernest Haycox

Just 95c each

Frontier Blood

Sixgun Duo

Starlight and Gunflame

Trigger Trio

CLIFTON ADAMS

Just 95c each

Hard Times & Arnie Smith

The Last Days of Wolf Garnett

The Badge and Harry Cole

Tragg's Choice

Once An Outlaw

The Reckless Men

The Grabhorn Bounty

Shorty

Available wherever paperbacks are sold or use this coupon.

ace books, (Dept. MM) Box 576, Times Square Station
New York. N.Y. 10036

Please send me titles checked above.

I enclose $ . . . . Add 35c handling fee per copy.

Name . . . .

Address . . . .

City . . . . State . . . . Zip . . . .

13E

NELSON NYE

04730	Bancroft Banco	$1.25
11161	The Clifton Contract	95¢
14196	Death Valley Slim	$1.25
30401	Gringo	75¢
30702	Gun Fued at Tiedown	$1.25
32726	Hellbound for Bellavat	$1.25
33100	Hideout Mountain	95¢
*37342	Iron Hand	75¢
43740	Kid from Lincoln County	$1.25
*48919	Long Run	75¢
49421	Lost Mine Named Salvation	95¢

Available wherever paperbacks are sold or use this coupon.

🖤 **ace books,** (Dept. MM) Box 576, Times Square Station
New York, N.Y. 10036

Please send me titles checked above.

I enclose $ . . . . Add 35c handling fee per copy.

Name . . . .

Address . . . .

City. . . . . State. . . . . Zip. . . . .

37D

T.V. OLSEN

*06331	Bitter Grass	95¢
31820	Haven of the Hunted	95¢
51850	The Man From Nowhere	95¢
53500	Mission To The West	$1.25
88010	Westward they Rode	$1.50

Available wherever paperbacks are sold or use this coupon.

ace books, (Dept. MM) Box 576. Times Square Station
New York, N.Y. 10036

Please send me titles checked above.

I enclose $.................. Add 35c handling fee per copy.

Name ....

Address ....

City..................... State............. Zip........

50C